KU-777-157

Road *to* Temptation

TERRA LITTLE

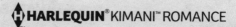

HARLEQUIN® KIMANI™ ROMANCE

ISBN-13: 978-0-373-86484-3

Road to Temptation

Printed in U.S.A.

H HARLEQUIN®
™ www.Harlequin.com

Terra Little has been reading romance novels for decades and falling in and out of love with the heroes within the book covers for just as long. When she's not in the classroom teaching English literature, you can most likely find her tucked away somewhere with her laptop, a dog-eared romance novel and romance so heavy on the brain that it somehow manages to weave its way into each and every story that she writes, regardless of the genre.

Terra resides in Missouri, but you can always find her on the web to share feedback, the occasional joke and suggestions for good reading at writeterralittle@yahoo.com.

Books by Terra Little

Harlequin Kimani Romance

Beneath Southern Skies
Road to Temptation

Visit the Author Profile page at
Harlequin.com for more titles.

For Alex.

Chapter 1

"I have a present for you," a sultry feline voice said, breaking the early-morning silence.

Elise Carrington looked up from her computer screen and frowned at the petite woman heading across the reception area in her direction. Curly sandy-brown hair with copper highlights flew wildly around her heart-shaped face and bounced against her shoulders with every step she took. Her plump lips were shellacked to perfection with a frosty fuchsia-tinted gloss and curved into a smile wide enough to sink the matching dimples in her cheeks. And the naturally arched brows above her deep-set, amber-colored eyes were poised, as if they expected to take flight at any moment.

Elise was immediately suspicious of the woman's intentions and slightly amused at the same time. Looking at another person and seeing an exact replica of herself still startled her every now and then, even though she'd been doing it for over thirty years and should've long since grown used to it. "Only you could manage to look bright and chipper at seven o'clock in the morning," she drawled, reaching for a mug of steaming coffee on the tabletop. "The rest of us poor schmucks are still cracking our eyelids open." She sipped the hot liquid gingerly, taking a moment to appreciate the creamy, caramel-flavored blend as she eyed her identical twin over the rim of the mug. She knew without having to be told that the file folder in her sister's hand didn't contain good news. The ones that tended to land in either of their laps these days rarely did. "What's up?"

"We have a runaway on our hands," Olivia Carrington said. "Well, I guess I should say *you* have a runaway on *your* hands."

"Excuse me?" Elise watched incredulously as Olivia smoothed her silk tunic over her hips, plopped into one of the upholstered chairs across the table from her and crossed her legs. The blouse's bright fuchsia color matched Olivia's lip gloss perfectly, reminding Elise that she hadn't bothered with anything more than leggings, a tunic-style hoodie and a fresh-scrubbed face this morning.

"I'm in the middle of the Donaldson case," her sister began, "but since you wrapped up your last case a few days ago, I figured that it was okay to accept a new case for you."

Elise's frown deepened. "That's my present? A new case?"

"Yep," Olivia chirped, dimpling prettily.

"Seriously. I don't know why I put up with you." Unconsciously mimicking her sibling's pose, Elise sat back in her chair and crossed her legs. "It's not like I don't have enough paperwork to do before I can finally close the file on my last case. Plus, I was hoping to take a break before I accepted another assignment, maybe sneak off to the Bahamas for a few days with a few of the girls and relax."

"Okay, first of all, you put up with me because we're twins. I'm two minutes older than you are, so you have to. Secondly, you don't have any *girls*. Plus, I couldn't have turned this one down if I wanted to and, believe me, I really wanted to. Do you remember Joel Barclay?"

"Sure, I remember Joel." How could she forget him? He and Olivia had carried on a scorching affair for several months back in high school. Despite the fact that he was twenty at the time, almost twenty-one, and a junior in college, and Olivia was barely seventeen and a high-school senior, what had started out as a carefree summer fling had quickly turned into an intense, nearly year-long relationship. Up to that point, Elise had never known a member of the opposite sex to hold Olivia's attention for longer than a few weeks at a time, and, as far as she knew, there had only been one or two others who'd managed to accomplish the feat since. It was a toss-up as to which of them—Joel or Elise—was more shocked when Olivia turned down Joel's marriage proposal and then broke up with him shortly afterward. "How is he?"

"He's on the verge of a nervous breakdown," Olivia

said, suddenly serious. "His daughter is missing, and we have to find her."

Surprised for the second time in as many minutes, Elise stared at her sister as she reached across the table for the file folder that Olivia held out to her. Setting her coffee aside, she opened the folder and scanned the 5x7 color photo that was clipped to a thin stack of written notes inside. The teenage girl staring back at her was the spitting image of the Joel she remembered—raven-haired, with classic features and a warm smile. According to the notes in the file, her name was Meagan, she had just turned eighteen a little over a month ago and she'd been missing for nearly twenty-four hours.

"I remember when he got married right after college," Elise remarked absently as she continued scanning the case notes. "You had the nerve to be upset because you weren't invited to the wedding, as if you hadn't just broken the poor guy's heart ten minutes before he walked down the aisle."

"It did seem like he got over me rather quickly, now that you mention it."

Elise's gaze flickered up to her sister's briefly and then skated away. No way was she touching *that* subject. Of the two of them, Olivia, bless her heart, was by far the vainest. As a teenager, Elise had always preferred the company of a good crime-fiction novel and a steaming mug of chamomile tea over that of chattering girls and hormonal boys. But Olivia was the exact opposite. She'd always been smart and had ultimately graduated cum laude from Loyola University, but only after their parents had spent most of their daughters' adolescent years worrying themselves sick over whether or not Olivia would ever get serious about something other than boys, lip gloss and gossip.

She'd also dated enough for the both of them in high school, which was just fine with Elise, since it had taken most of the pressure of adolescent expectations off her. But Olivia's tendency to make everything about herself could be a bit much if you didn't know her well enough to know that her heart was just as big as her head.

"So this is their kid, huh?"

"Their one and only," Olivia said. "So you can see why I couldn't say no to the case, but I couldn't exactly take it on myself, right? It would be…weird."

"Yes, I can see how it might be."

It was a high-profile case, one that would definitely get its fifteen minutes worth of fame if the media caught wind of it. After marrying his pregnant rebound girlfriend right out of college, Joel had set his sights on a career in politics and law. He was currently in his first term as a circuit court judge, a seat that he'd just barely won in the last election, thanks to his teenage daughter's penchant for scandalous public exploits. Add that to the fact that, before he'd become a judge, he was the kind of young brash defense attorney who himself had a tendency to take on the kinds of controversial cases that kept him in the public eye, and the result was a private life that didn't exactly lend itself to voter sympathy. The last thing he or his wife needed was the kind of publicity that a presumably out-of-control runaway child would attract, especially since his name was now on the short list for appointment to the Illinois Appellate Court. That had to be why he'd bitten the bullet and reached out to Olivia. His was just the kind of case that Carrington Consulting specialized in.

In the three years since Elise and Olivia had grown tired of taking orders from power-hungry men and gone into business for themselves, they'd taken on countless missing persons cases and, at last tally, they were operating at a more than 90 percent success rate. With Elise's background in law enforcement and Olivia's forensic experience, if anyone could find Meagan quickly and with a minimum of fuss, they could.

Glancing at her watch, Elise pushed back from the table and got to her feet. She picked up her laptop, coffee mug and, as a last thought, the file. "I hate to run out on you like this, sis, but I have a videoconference later this morning," she told Olivia. "Can I finish looking over the notes on the case right afterward and let you know what I decide?"

"This afternoon?" Olivia's eyes widened in alarm as she tracked Elise's progress out of the room. "Joel was frantic when he called this morning, Elise. I don't know if putting this off until this afternoon is such a good idea." Her wispy hair rode the wind as she swiveled in her chair. "He mentioned something about her having behavioral problems. Something could happen to her by then, if it hasn't already."

Elise thought about the possibility for a moment. "I won't be long," she said before disappearing down the hallway.

"Okay, but if your videoconference isn't until this

afternoon, where are you going now? It's still morning," Olivia called after her.

"I have a teleconference in ten minutes, and I can't miss it. My last case isn't going to close itself," Elise called back. "When the phone rings, it'll probably be for me, so I'll pick up the extension in the study."

Hoping that she had escaped having to make a decision on the Barclay case, if only for a little while, Elise closed the study door at her back and took a seat at the conference table across the room. She was almost done setting up her temporary base of operations when Olivia opened the door and stuck her head inside the room. Elise couldn't say that she was all that surprised.

"I have an idea. Why don't I have Harriet call Joel and set up a meeting with him for this afternoon?" she said, referring to the gray-haired dynamo who was their administrative assistant. "Just in case," she added when Elise's amber gaze rose from the computer screen to meet hers and narrowed in warning.

"You're not going to let up until I agree to take this case, are you?"

"Why do you ask questions that you already know the answers to?"

"All right," she said, nodding reluctantly. "All right. Have Harriet schedule an early-evening meeting. I should be done with everything by then, so I'll go to him instead of having him come here. I need some fresh air, anyway. But I'm telling you, after this case, I'm officially on vacation."

She looked away from Olivia's smiling face when the phone rang. Pushing a button to accept the call, she didn't see the victory fist pump that Olivia executed before the door closed softly in her wake.

Working from home did have its advantages, Elise mused as she stepped into the shower and quickly soaped herself from head to toe. It certainly made transitioning from one task to the next on her to-do list a lot easier. Ironically enough, that was precisely the argument that Olivia had used three years ago when the question of where they would set up Carrington Consulting's business offices had come up. Elise was in favor of leasing office space in downtown St. Louis, so they could at least try to keep their private investigations business and their personal lives separate, but Olivia's arguments to the contrary had eventually worn her down. There was more than enough room in the house for both business and pleasure to coexist, she'd pointed out, and they could save money on overhead expenses. Put that way, Elise could hardly refuse. Olivia was right on both counts, though Elise would cut out her tongue before she'd admit it.

Her parents had built the house five years ago, after her father decided to give up his thriving Clayton law practice and retire early, and, for a while, decorating it had kept both Lance and Yolanda Carrington busy. It was a showplace, something tangible that they could both appreciate and enjoy after years of hard work. It wasn't until after it was finally completed and each room had been meticulously appointed that her parents had suddenly decided that they didn't want to live there, after all. Almost thirty years of living in the States was long enough, her father had said. He was homesick for London, where he'd been born and raised. Leaving the house to their daughters, they had updated their passports, packed up their personal belongings and left the country seemingly in the blink of an eye, a decision that hadn't surprised Olivia at all but that had finally confirmed for Elise the origin of Olivia's flighty tendencies.

True to form, Olivia hadn't wasted any time ditching her South County condo and moving in, but Elise hadn't been quite so eager to let go of her Clayton town house. Her sister had already been living in the house a full six months before she sublet her town house and joined her.

After showering and moisturizing, she paired a cream-colored cashmere sweater dress with a wide chocolate-brown belt and matching suede boots. The steam from the shower had completely wrung the life out of her hair, so she brushed it until it was smooth and caught her wild, curly locks at the crown of her head with a jeweled clip. As a finishing touch, she added mascara and gold-tinted lip gloss before tossing her cell phone and iPad in her red Kate Spade tote and slipping her favorite Chanel sunglasses over her eyes.

Downstairs in the foyer, she grabbed a red vintage leather coat from the coat closet and then swiped her car keys from the entry table on her way out the door. With just about forty-five minutes to spare, she could just barely make it to Joel Barclay's Waterloo, Illinois, estate on time.

Chapter 2

Half an hour later, Elise's Jaguar was stuck in rush-hour traffic on Interstate 40, sandwiched between an ancient bright green Beetle that had obscene bumper stickers plastered all over it, and a snarling black Hummer with tinted windows and aggressive tendencies. Every few minutes, the Beetle crept forward a couple of feet, putting her that much closer to the exit she wanted, which, thankfully, was only about a half mile up ahead. Thanks to the pushy Hummer that had been riding her rear bumper nonstop for the last twenty minutes, a half mile seemed more like a million. The thing practically growled every time she hit the brakes and forced it to stop on a dime barely an inch from her bumper, as if her car and her car alone was responsible for the bumper-to-bumper traffic.

Jerk. She eyed the idling bully in her rearview mirror steadily. The windows weren't just tinted, they were also reflective, making it completely impossible to see who, or, in this case, *what* was inside, behind the wheel. But she didn't need to actually see the face of evil to know that it existed, did she? He—and she was convinced that it was a *he*—was probably one of those corporate types, with a string of vengeful ex-wives, dangerously high blood pressure and out-of-control anger issues. He probably laughed maniacally every time that his rolling bully narrowly avoided tagging her bumper because driving like a maniac and terrorizing everyone else on the road made him feel powerful.

Elise docked her iPod into the dashboard, scrolled through her music and selected her Marsha Ambrosius playlist. Turning up the volume a couple of notches, she sat back in her seat and drummed her fingers on the steering wheel in time to the rhythm. She couldn't remember the last time that she'd been nervous about anything.

Before Carrington Consulting, she'd been a police officer for two years and then a US marshal for seven, and, by now, there was very little about criminal behavior that surprised her. She'd dealt with bullies every day on the job, and most of them were men who were on the same side of the badge that she'd been on. Compared to that particular brand of chaos, this maniac and his souped-up Hummer were child's play. Still, his theatrics were starting to get on her nerves, especially since she was in just as much of a hurry to get where she was going as he apparently was.

I'm stuck in traffic, she texted Harriet. Please contact the Barclays and advise them that I'm going to be—

A car horn blared behind her, calling her attention to the fact that the Beetle had moved forward in front of her just about a fraction of an inch. She rolled her eyes at the culprit in her rearview mirror, then slowly caught up to the Beetle, with the Hummer riding her rear bumper the entire time. Its tires squealed when it suddenly stopped behind her and she sighed long and hard.

—a little late, she finished texting. She was *this close* to her exit. Another fifty yards, give or take, and she could ditch the Hummer from hell for good. Waiting for the moment that she could escape was like watching paint dry.

Done, Harriet texted back a few minutes later.

As soon as Elise was close enough to maneuver her Jaguar into the exit lane, she did, stirring up roadside gravel in her wake as she gratefully left the standing traffic on the interstate and took off down the exit ramp. Resisting the urge to flip the bird to her rearview mirror as she went, she rolled to a stop at the red light at the bottom of the ramp and reached for her cell phone, intending to reactivate the GPS.

She didn't see the Hummer bearing down on her until it was too late to do anything except stare up at her rearview mirror in disbelief. "What in the world?" She heard tires squealing and then a sharp bump from behind sent her Jaguar hopping forward on the pavement and her cell phone flying out of her hand. Her car shuddered to a stop dangerously close to the Buick in front of it and vibrated with indignation for several seconds afterward.

Oh my God! I've just been hit by a stalker! Frantic, Elise threw her car into Park and quickly dived at the passenger-side floorboard in search of her cell phone.

The light changed, and, as if nothing out of the ordinary had just occurred, the line of cars to her left moved forward and merged into traffic, while the Hummer behind her pulled into the tow lane to her right and its driver shut off its engine. It took a second for the gravity of the situation to sink in, but when it did, she joined him in the tow lane, leaving enough space between the two vehicles to make a quick escape possible.

It didn't occur to her to be afraid. What she was, she suddenly decided, was completely and thoroughly pissed.

Hidden behind tinted one-way glass, Broderick Cannon saw the woman coming, closing the distance between her sophisticated little gold car and his Hummer with long-legged, angry strides. With every step she took, her leather coat flapped open, giving him an enticing glimpse of nipples hard enough to cut glass underneath her dress and a generous hourglass figure. He sat back in his seat and lazily watched her come, wondering what the Jackie O–style sunglasses covering half of her face were hiding and if she was packing something other than lipstick in the ridiculously large purse dangling from the crook of her arm. She had to be, he decided, pressing a button to disengage the electronic locks and then releasing his seat belt. Either that or she was certifiable.

The pretty ones always are, he thought as his gaze momentarily settled on the rhythmic sway of her hips, then slowly traveled back up to her face. The fact that she could be, this very second, walking into a dangerous trap either hadn't occurred to her or she simply didn't care. Either way, the chances of her being completely nuts were looking better and better.

As if she could somehow read his thoughts, she slowed to a stop at the midway point between their vehicles and struck a pose, tapping a foot impatiently on the pavement. He cracked a smile despite himself. She was a sitting duck, and she didn't even know it. But just in case she wasn't as stylishly clueless as she looked in her red-bottom boots, he released the safety on his .357 SIG Sauer pistol and tucked it into the rear waistband of his slacks. Twice, he'd seen her touching up her makeup in the rearview mirror, *instead of driving.* Another time, she'd held up traffic while she fiddled with something on the dashboard *instead of driving.* And still another time, she'd spent way too much time fiddling with her cell phone *instead of driving.* Any idiot could see that her negligence was to blame for their accident, but maybe forcing him to rear-end her was her plan all along. Maybe she thought that *he* was the sitting duck.

And maybe pigs really do fly, Broderick thought as he climbed down from the Hummer and went to meet her.

Fifteen years ago, he'd put away his master's degree in computer engineering from Brown University, and, instead of heading for Silicon Valley like he'd always planned, he joined the navy and applied to the SEALs program. He was recruited by the CIA's Special Operations Group a few months after graduation, and the rest was history.

His specialties were global threat suppression and hostage extraction, and, for the past fifteen years, that's exactly what he'd done—brought home hostages that the rest of the world had written off as hopelessly lost; hunted down reclusive global leaders and brought them to justice; and gathered intelligence on terrorist sleeper cells worldwide. Aside from the fact that he was a fifth-degree black belt, a decorated marksman and fluent in three languages, he was damn good at his job and, somewhere, he had a chest full of medals and commendations to prove it. As a result, when he decided to go into reserve status three years ago and launch Cannon Corp as the initial phase of his eventual transition back into civilian life, his inaugural client list had damn near built itself. Most of the cases that he took on nowadays were significantly less risky than the ones he'd once lived and breathed around the clock, but he hadn't yet learned how to adjust his actions and reactions accordingly, and he wasn't sure he ever would.

Nevertheless, one thing was for damn sure—he'd never been anyone's sitting duck.

"You hit my car!" she shrieked as soon as he emerged from the Hummer and sent the door flying shut behind him. Another round of cars whipped past them just in time to catch the tail end of her accusation, complete with flailing arms and a perfectly shocked O of a mouth. He barely resisted the urge to roll his eyes to the sky.

The pretty ones were always drama queens, too.

"Are you out of your mind?" he countered calmly, approaching her head-on. "Or does the fact that you seem to have no regard for your personal safety mean that's already a foregone conclusion?" To her credit, she didn't flinch when he stopped less than a foot away from her, dropped his hands on his hips and purposely loomed over her. Instead, she crossed her arms underneath those lovely, Jell-O–like breasts of hers, shifted her weight to one side and faced him defiantly. She was taller than he'd first thought, and up close, her glittering mouth was nothing short of amazing.

"That's funny because I was about to ask you the same thing. I could've sworn that road rage is illegal."

He looked up from staring at her shimmering lips and found the foggy outline of her eyes behind her dark lenses. "So is texting while driving," he fired back. "And if touching up your makeup while driving isn't already illegal, it certainly should be. Don't you think?"

An outraged chuckle burst out of her mouth. "You know, I think that what should be illegal," she said without missing a beat, "is driving around in a pimped-out monstrosity, hiding behind tinted windows while you terrorize every other vehicle on the road. Don't you think?"

His head started shaking in denial right around the time that she referred to his baby as a pimped-out monstrosity, and it was still shaking when he said, "Not quite every *other* vehicle on the road, just little toy ones being driven by Barbie dolls who can't stop looking at themselves in the rearview mirror long enough to properly operate them." That pimped-out monstrosity crack had stung.

Her mouth dropped open, snapped closed and then dropped open again. The process was fascinating to watch.

"*Excuse me?* I'm not the maniac who rammed into the back of someone else's car. You are."

"I think you might be using the word *rammed* a little loosely here, because—"

"You did ram my car! Are you denying it?"

"I don't think so and no, I'm not denying that there was some contact between your vehicle and mine. What I'm saying is that I merely *tapped* your rear bumper. I didn't ram it."

"There's a scratch."

"No, there isn't."

"Yes, there is."

"I don't believe you. Show me."

"Are you kidding me? You can't seriously believe that I...that you...that..." She floundered visibly, then stopped short, throwing up her hands in defeat and sucking in a slow, steady breath. "You know what? Whatever. This is pointless," she said, waving a dismissive hand in his general direction and then spinning around on her skyscraper heels. "I've already called the police, and they should be here soon," she tossed back at him over her shoulder as she walked off. "I'm going to wait for them over there. You stay here."

Her butt was a work of art. "Fine," he called after her, staring at it.

"Fine!" she yelled back.

Okay, so maybe the Barbie doll crack was a low blow. But it wasn't like she was the only one who had a reason to be irritated. Visiting the Midwest in late February had to rank in the top five on Broderick's personal list of things that would never occur to a sane person. Yet here he was, and the circumstances that had brought him here weren't even close to being the best. There were no guarantees on how long he could actually stay, so every second counted. It stood to reason that he hadn't bothered to factor time into his already-tight schedule for dealing with distracted women drivers and the traffic accidents that they inevitably caused.

And now that his schedule was shot to hell because of one such driver, she was giving *him* attitude when *he* was the one who should be furious? *What the hell ever.* She was over there right now, inspecting her bumper like it was in danger of falling off. Taking picture after picture of it with her laptop-sized cell phone, from as many different angles as she could manage, in case he was thinking about running back to his Hummer before the police arrived and fleeing the scene. She had no idea that, as far as traffic accidents went, she should've been happy that he was the one who'd rammed her toy car and not some psychotic maniac, because a scratch on her bumper could've ended up being the very least of her worries.

Just last month, his firm had been called in to investigate a kidnapping that had gone horribly wrong long before someone thought to refer the young woman's distraught parents to him. After nearly a week of local police and FBI involvement, it had taken his men just over two days to find the girl, but by then the only thing that their discovery could offer her parents and local police was closure. That and the identity of her kidnapper— a psychopath who, among other things, had regularly staged minor traffic accidents to lure unsuspecting women into his sadistic trap. It was how he'd gotten their daughter, his last victim.

Minor traffic infractions just like this one. And un- suspecting women just like the one snapping pictures right now.

Where the hell were the police, anyway?

Against his better judgment, he walked over to where she was leaning back against the passenger door of her Jaguar, working her cell phone like a speed demon, to find out. When his shadow fell over her, she looked up, saw him standing there and uttered the sexiest sigh that he'd ever heard. Somewhere along the shaft of his semi- sleeping penis, a nerve yawned and stretched.

Tongue in cheek, he said, "Excuse me, but when you said you'd already called the police, you did mean today, right?" He didn't need to actually see her eyes to know that she rolled them.

Hard.

"Of course I called them today. Trust me, I would not be standing here indulging your obvious mental instability if I wasn't absolutely certain that they were on the way."

The tiny diamond stud in her left nostril was a sparkling stranger in a landscape of even tinier cocoa- colored freckles sprinkled across the bridge of her nose. It, unlike her forked tongue, was attractive, he thought as a grin played with his lips. "I'm sorry, but did you just call me unstable?"

"I believe so, yes," she said, dropping her cell phone into her purse and then taking out a makeup compact. She flipped it open and inspected her lip gloss critically. "If I'd known exactly how unstable, I would've locked myself inside my car from the very beginning and called in the National Guard, instead."

"Which reminds me," Broderick sniped back at her without missing a beat. "In situations like this, that's precisely what you should do. Another time, you might consider staying inside your car while you wait for the police or anyone else to arrive. I'm just saying," he quickly added when she bristled visibly. "If I were, say, a serial killer, you would have just walked right into my trap."

"*Are* you a serial killer?"

He wished he could see her eyes. "Fortunately for you, no, I'm not."

"Well, that's a relief."

"Isn't it?"

Five months, Broderick suddenly remembered as he watched her lips form the words that she spoke. That's how long it'd been since he last made time in his schedule or room in his bed for a woman. Five months.

Crazy work hours, dangerous working conditions and near-constant travel. They were all to blame for his forced celibacy. Mostly, anyway. In his line of work, maintaining a relationship was like being burdened with a second job, especially since he was never really off duty from the first one. There was no such thing as a typical assignment, set time frames or guaranteed outcomes, and he liked it that way. Women? Not so much, especially since those same improbabilities applied to his personal life, as well. He had long since made peace with the fact that his career choice meant that he'd probably die a lonely old man, but in the meantime, he'd been known to occasionally carve out a little time for a no-strings-attached fling.

He wondered if she'd be willing to join him. Then he said, "You know, the fact that you can joke about your personal safety is very telling. A random encounter like this one, on the interstate—any interstate—could've ended very differently for you."

"Then I guess it's lucky for you that it didn't, Mr...?"

"Cannon. Broderick Cannon." He made himself look away from her mouth. "And you are?"

"Quite capable of defending myself, Mr. Cannon."

Her glistening lips curved into a smile so charming and so innocently sweet that every nerve in his penis simultaneously sputtered. His gaze wandered back down to her mouth just as twin dimples sank into her cheeks, a third one winked out at him from the center of her chin and a soft giggle eased out from between even, white teeth. A second later, it flickered back up, locked on to the dim of her eyes behind her dark lenses and narrowed speculatively.

"And, oh, look!" she exclaimed in a childlike voice. "Just in case you really *are* a serial killer, here come the police. I feel safer already." Sidestepping around him carefully, she walked off and left him standing there with visions of his tongue dancing between her thighs flashing before his eyes.

It wasn't until a half hour later, when their fender bender had been duly documented and his was the last vehicle to drive away from the scene, that Broderick took the time to look at her insurance information and the business card that she'd grudgingly handed him before jumping into her car and speeding away. It was printed on soft pink parchment paper and lightly scented. He'd been too busy staring at her to pay it much attention before then.

Her name, he thought as he wondered exactly what kind of fly-by-night operation Carrington Consulting was, was Elise Carrington.

Chapter 3

Classical music was billowing from underneath the study doors, filling the dimly lit foyer, when Elise finally made it home. Knowing that her sister was undoubtedly in the midst of it and hoping to avoid running into her just yet, Elise closed the door as quietly as she could and tiptoed to the coat closet to hang up her coat. After the ridiculous afternoon she'd just had, the last thing she was in the mood for was one of her sister's nerve-jangling inquisitions. The drive home was stressful enough as it was, without having to get into a whole *thing* with Olivia as soon as she walked through the door. Right now, all she wanted to do was change into something loose and comfortable, get her hands on a couple of aspirin and then wash them down with a glass of white wine. She'd come clean to Olivia later.

Under the cover of Tchaikovsky's urgent-sounding crescendos, Elise began creeping toward the staircase at the far end of the foyer. Holding her breath and moving on the tips of her toes, she narrowly avoided teetering sideways into the centerpiece of the foyer—a marble, French baroque-style pedestal table—by a hair and froze for five long seconds. Satisfied that Olivia hadn't heard her, she started carefully inching forward again. She had almost reached the bottom step when the volume of the music suddenly dropped, one of the study doors swung open and Olivia appeared in the doorway like an apparition. Caught, Elise stopped short and slowly removed her sunglasses.

Great. Just great.

"Soooo…" Olivia said in a singsong voice as she leaned in the doorway and eyed Elise balefully over the rim of her reading glasses. "Joel called."

"I figured he would. What did he say?" As if she didn't already know.

"He said that you walked into his house, stayed just long enough to decline his case and then walked right back out. And then you were in some sort of road-rage incident that led to a car accident?" Arms still folded and eyebrows raised, Olivia padded barefoot across the foyer until she was close enough to see Elise clearly in the muted lighting. Circling her slowly, she looked her up and down with a wrinkle of concern creasing her forehead.

"What are you doing?" Elise asked, tracking her movements suspiciously.

"I'm making sure you're okay. The way Joel was

going on and on, it was like listening to an episode of *How to Get Away with Murder*. I was worried sick. What in the world happened to you after you left here earlier?"

"Well, Joel was right about one thing. There was an accident but—"

"*What?* Oh my God, what happened?" Eyes wide, she pounced on Elise, checking with searching hands for possible bumps, bruises or breaks. Finding none, she breathed an audible sigh of relief. "Are you hurt?"

"I'm fine," Elise said, warding off Olivia's hovering hands as she moved around her and reached for the wooden banister behind her. "It was really just a tap, and it happened on my way to Joel's house, not after I left. I'm surprised Joel even knew about it." She climbed one step, then two and then it occurred to her. "Wait, what am I saying? Of course, Joel knew about it. He probably told him all about it before I got there."

"*He?* Who's *he* and exactly what was there to tell?"

Elise opened her mouth to explain, then thought better of it. Introducing Broderick Cannon's name into the conversation right now would only result in more questions, and, if Elise factored in the questions that were already in queue to be asked, they could end up standing there half the night, which was so out of the question that it was laughable. There was only so much harassment that she was willing to take in one day, without a chilled glass of Reisling on hand as backup, and she'd reached her threshold well over an hour ago.

"Elise?" Olivia prompted with a cocked brow when the silence stretched from one second into five.

"Just some friend of Joel's from college. No one important," Elise explained vaguely, impatiently. "A private investigator, I think."

And a demigod, she silently added, mentally reviewing Broderick's finer points in her mind. Six-three or -four, with the kind of imposing build that was best served scantily clad and glistening with body oil. Smooth, mocha brown skin, full lips and sleepy-looking bedroom eyes, rimmed with long black lashes. A deliberate five-o'clock shadow that was as expertly groomed as his close-cropped black hair was and a slightly off-kilter smile that, by itself, was seemingly harmless but that, together with the whole of him, was exactly the thing that instantly melted a woman's panties and summarily dismissed every ounce of her self-control.

Elise knew because she'd been transfixed herself by the way his protruding Adam's apple bobbed rhythmically in his powerful-looking neck as he talked and the way the slashes in his cheeks bracketed his mouth just so when he smiled. She'd been secretly appreciating the way the muscles in his forearms strained against the sleeves of his black trench coat whenever he moved his arms, when she also happened to notice that he wasn't wearing a wedding ring and suddenly thought, *eighteen months.* That's how much time had passed since her last relationship ended and, not until the moment that Broderick loomed over her and blithely suggested that he could be a serial killer, had it ever occurred to her to question exactly why.

At some point, very early on, when she was still thinking clearly and in her right mind, she noticed the look in his eyes, recognized it for what it was and knew she was in trouble. The same X-rated thoughts that were running through her mind were clearly running through his, but, unlike her, he didn't seem to care that she could see them. She should've been offended by the unobstructed view into his carnal thoughts, but, instead, she was excited and slippery wet, and embarrassed by her body's reaction to him. And, honestly, she'd been too busy ogling him right back and thanking God for dark sunglasses to hide behind while she did it, to bother jumping on anyone's feminist soapbox. Frankly, his boldness, his tendency to stare at her mouth when she talked and at her breasts when he thought she wasn't looking, turned her on.

He was a spectacular-looking man, an interesting cross between Boris Kodjoe and the Terminator, with a hint of something else lurking beneath the surface, something other than his amazing looks and tall, powerhouse physique. He'd been dressed like a business mogul, in a flawlessly tailored trench coat, cashmere dress slacks and hand-sewn Italian loafers. But the energy around him was raw and intense, his gait controlled and predatory, like a caged beast, one that was chomping at the bit and impatiently biding his time on lockdown.

My God, he was sexy.

Elise had never been more attracted to a man in her entire life.

But that information was on a need-to-know basis, and, as far as Elise was concerned, Olivia didn't need to know. They were identical twins, but when it came to men, the two of them were like Jekyll and Hyde. Olivia was a femme fatale, with a trail of broken hearts in her wake that dated all the way back to kindergarten to prove it. While Elise…well, Elise had simply watched the drama that was her sister's life unfold from the sidelines. She was a bookworm, who'd been obsessed with maintaining her position as captain of the debate team and with maintaining at least a 3.5 GPA at all times. She was seventeen, almost eighteen, when she got around to her first tongue kiss and a whopping twenty-one when she fumbled her way through losing her virginity, and even then she'd only done it because she figured that it was about time. To this day, she could count on one hand the number of men that she'd been intimate with since then.

And she'd still have two fingers left.

Men like Broderick Cannon scared the hell out of her.

"Wait, so Joel hired another firm?" Olivia wanted to know. "A competing firm?"

"I didn't really leave him any choice. After he hit me, I—"

Olivia gasped. "*What?* Joel *hit* you?"

"No," Elise cried impatiently, stretching the word out into five long syllables. Just a few minutes ago, escape had seemed so possible. Now? Not so much. "Joel didn't hit me, Broderick Cannon did. Please try to keep up."

"I am trying, but you're not making it very easy," Olivia said, laying a hand on Elise's forehead and looking concerned. "You seem rattled, and you're a little flushed, too. Are you sure you're okay?"

Elise rolled her eyes to the ceiling and swatted Olivia's

hand away. "Stop that. Of course I'm okay." She climbed two more steps. "I just need a few minutes—"

"Well, at least come into the kitchen with me and have some tea. It should be done steeping by now. It'll help you relax, and you can tell me all about whatever happened today…from the beginning and in chronological order this time. How about that?"

—*alone to catch my breath and process everything*, Elise finished silently. Aloud, she said: "Well—" The ringing doorbell cut her off. For a second, she was torn between hanging around to see who was at the door and getting out while the getting was good. "Who could *that* be at this time of the evening?"

Olivia frowned at her watch. "I don't know. Maybe it's the courier that Eli was supposed to send over with some papers five hours ago," she said, referring to Eli Seamus, the retired CIA agent who moonlighted as their Competitive Intelligence Analyst, or CIA, and all-around computer hacker. "He's called five times now, each time to let me know that he was running a little later than he was running when he called the time before that."

"Who? Eli?"

"No, the courier, and you can bet Eli is going to hear all about it first thing in the morning." The doorbell rang again, and Olivia's neck rolled ominously. "He's five hours late, and *I'm* the one who's taking too long?" She threw up her hands and let them fall back to her sides wearily. "Incredible." Sighing disgustedly, she whirled and headed for the door, giving Elise just the opportunity that she needed to hurry up the rest of the stairs. "Listen, don't go anywhere, okay?" Olivia called out to Elise as she switched on the veranda light and went up on her tiptoes to peek through the peephole. "I'm still not convinced that you're completely okay, and I want to talk some more about what happened today."

Elise decided to go with getting out while the getting was good and made a dash for it, heading up a second, shorter flight of stairs to the second-floor balcony that overlooked the foyer while Olivia was still talking. She leaned over the balcony and called back, "Sure, I'll be right back," then hurried down the east hallway to her bedroom suite and firmly shut the door behind her.

In about an hour, she thought a few minutes later, as she peeled off her clinging panties and stepped into a cold shower.

Chapter 4

The massive entry door swung open, and Broderick's brown eyes met a pair of gorgeous amber-colored ones. She'd gotten rid of the giant sunglasses and traded her dress and boots for tight black pants, a flowing top that bared one caramel-colored shoulder, and bare feet. Up top, a pair of eyeglasses was anchored in the midst of the wild, curly lion's mane framing her face, and, down below, glossy, hot-pink toenails and an ultrafeminine diamond ankle bracelet winked up at him. If it hadn't been for the subtle, provocative gleam in her eye, she could've passed for an innocent college coed, with her smooth, clear skin and big, blinking eyes. She was so completely opposite of the snarling sex kitten from earlier that, for a second, he wondered if he was looking at the same person. Then she smiled and he thought, *There she is.*

"Well?" she said. "Are you going to speak first or should I?"

"I guess I should, since you walked out of our last meeting before I had a chance to fully explain myself." She had the nerve to cock a brow at his tone but damned if he cared. She knew damn well why he was there and exactly what he wanted, and if his tone was sharp, she knew why that was, as well—*because he was on the verge of shaking her until her teeth rattled around in her head like loose marbles.*

Anticipating another round of pointless sparring, he put up a hand to ward her off and tried for a more diplomatic tone. "Look, obviously, I had no idea who you were when we met earlier, and, for the record, I didn't figure out what Joel was up to until right after I arrived at his estate, which was about five minutes before you did. If I'd known beforehand, we wouldn't even be having this conversation. But since I am here and the circumstances surrounding Meagan's disappearance are less than ideal, I came here to ask you to please reconsider Joel's and my proposal."

He expected her to start hissing and spitting at him again, but she surprised him, instead, with a thoughtful expression and a few seconds of contemplative silence. "Joel's proposal?" she asked, pursing lips that begged to be sucked and staring at him through narrowed eyes. "Sounds interesting. Go on." She leaned against the door casually and waited.

"I'd be glad to but could we talk inside?" The temperature had dropped to somewhere between twenty and twenty-five degrees in a matter of hours and, the later it got, the more brisk the wind became. Supposedly, it was an unseasonably warm midwestern February, but to Broderick, who'd grown up on the West Coast, anything below seventy degrees was cruel and unusual punishment. He couldn't wait to get the hell out of Dodge.

"Sorry, but no. You're a complete stranger, so right here works for me." She giggled at his pithy expression and then gave him one right back. "So what was it that you wanted me to reconsider, again?"

"As I said before, I wasn't expecting that Joel would hire you to find Meagan and then want us to work together, but now that I'm here and the idea is on the table, I think we should seriously consider it."

"Oh?" She cocked a brow. "Why?"

"Meagan is my goddaughter, and while this isn't the first time she's run off, it is the first time she's run off without her medication. We believe she's with a guy that she's been dating behind her parents' backs for the past couple of months. His name is Peter Danforth, as in the son of state senator Frank Danforth."

"I see, and are Peter's parents searching for him, as well?"

"Apparently, they flee to the Caribbean when it's wintertime here. But we do know that their son is a grad student at Mizzou, who just happens to be well over the age of twenty-one, and, according to the family's housekeeper, present and accounted for on campus as we speak. So, technically, he isn't missing and I, for one, couldn't care less about him right now. Frankly, I'd have hung up on Joel when he called me late last night, if it wasn't for the fact that Meagan was diagnosed with bipolar disorder a month ago and she's been refusing treatment. Let's just say that her decision-making skills are questionable under the best of circumstances. Factor in a rich boyfriend with a valid ID, platinum credit cards and mental illness, and she's a ticking time bomb. As of about fifteen minutes ago, she was in the Jefferson City area, which isn't very far away, but based on her travel pattern so far, it doesn't look like she's planning to head back in this direction any time soon. I could be wrong, but I'd rather go after her now than have something that could've been prevented happen later, because I didn't."

"I get that part," she said, looking slightly confused. "But what I don't get is why you need a partner. You seem to have a handle on things already."

"Ordinarily I wouldn't, but I'm in the middle of another case right now and there's a possibility that I could be called away without notice. I'd like to have an associate with me in case that happens, someone who could pick up the slack, if necessary."

"You mean like a sidekick?"

He shrugged. "That's one way of putting it, but—" He realized his mistake a second too late, when her expression went from open and curious to closed for business in the blink of an eye. "If I might rephrase—"

"No need. I think I understand perfectly, Mr…"

That made him laugh. "Oh, so now you don't remember my name?"

She looked taken aback. "Is there a reason why I should?"

Was she serious? Just a few hours ago, he'd been positive that something interesting was happening between them, something that, if played right, would eventually lead to her straddling him and riding his stiff, swollen cock until they were both out of breath. He wanted her, and, underneath her prickly exterior, he thought he'd sensed a mutual attraction. But now, standing face-to-face with her again, without so much as a spark between them, he reminded himself that there was always room for error, and, though it didn't happen often, he wasn't above entertaining the strong possibility that he'd made one. Either that or he'd been right all along and she really was nuts, in which case he was probably talking to one of her multiple personalities.

"No, I guess not," Broderick conceded after several seconds of holding up his end of a staring contest. "Look, about Joel's proposal…"

"It sounds like what you need is an assistant, and I'm afraid that's something we can't help you with. I could, however, recommend a couple of our past interns who might be available for a last-minute assignment like this, if you'd like."

The emphasis that she'd placed on *last minute* hadn't escaped his notice, but he wasn't in the mood to rise to the bait. He'd wasted enough time already. "I have an entire staff of assistants at my disposal, Elise. The last thing I need is another one." Something flickered in her eyes when he said her name, but it came and went so quickly that he wasn't sure if he'd actually seen it or if it was a trick of the light.

"Fine, so use one of them," she suggested and he thought, for a tense millisecond, that he saw it again.

"I would if it was that simple," he said, and the sigh she offered in response was soft and wistful, sexy in a breezy, nonchalant kind of way that irritated the hell out of him. He rolled right over it. "But the thing is, both cases require extreme discretion. Meagan's case, in particular, needs to be kept away from both the press and local law enforcement, for obvious reasons. So far, that hasn't been much of an issue, but if her behavior were to escalate and she were to become a threat to herself or others, because she was off her meds and not thinking clearly, then who knows how things could play out."

"Okay, but I still don't understand what any of these situations you mentioned have to do with me." Now it was Broderick's turn to sigh and he did, deeply, impatiently and borderline rudely, a fact that she seemed to find funny.

He hated wasting time, particularly when lives could be at stake, and he especially hated having to explain himself when it came to his business and how he chose to handle it. In his line of work, every second counted and, so far, Elise Carrington had already caused him to squander so many of them that he'd lost track. And, like an idiot, he had let her. She was right. It wasn't like the fate of the world relied on whether or not she helped him. Truthfully, he'd move much faster and cover much more ground without her slowing him down. She was beautiful, but he wasn't under any illusions about the scope of her professional capabilities. Her expensive, scented business card had introduced her as a *Private Investigations Consultant*, whatever the hell *that* was. But based on her red-bottom boots, painted-on designer clothing and the mini-mansion that she called home, it was way more likely that she spent most of her time trailing cheating husbands and reporting back to disillusioned housewives. Which meant that her skill set, or lack thereof, as the case likely was, was a liability that he could've happily done without. He was surprised that Joel had sought assistance from someone like her in the first place.

Clearly Joel's anxious mental state had compromised his thought process but what the hell was Broderick's problem? The jury might've still been out on whether or not *she* was certifiable, but the longer he stood there, spinning his wheels and ogling her on the sly, he wondered if maybe he had it all wrong and *he* was actually the crazy one.

"They have everything to do with you because, thanks to you and the traffic accident you caused, I don't have time to vet another candidate. As it is, I should've been in Jefferson City hours ago. If I had been, I'd probably be on my way back here with Meagan right now and none of this would even be an issue. But, since it is an issue and Joel has apparently already vetted you, I think an appropriate gesture of professional goodwill would be for you to accept the case and see it through."

She stared at him for several seconds—a wide-eyed, stunned stare that he was compelled to return full measure—and then she reached up, plucked her glasses out of her hair and slipped them over her eyes. Behind the spotless lenses, her eyes were narrowed and searching. "You're saying that your failure to plan accordingly is my fault?"

"What I'm saying is that Joel and I need your help."

"Well, I'm sorry, but Carrington Consulting has a very strict policy against partnerships with outside entities," she informed him tartly, her eyes still narrowed and, now, a hand on her hip. "So, while I can appreciate your dilemma, I can't violate policy."

"Can't or won't?"

She hesitated for a moment, then rolled her eyes heavenward as if to say, *hey, what can we do?* Then she mouthed the word *sorry* to him, stepped back and began closing the door in his face.

Let her go, his mind screamed at the same time that his foot shot out and breached the threshold at the last possible second. He hadn't planned on going into detail about the other case that he was working on because it was none of her business. But the bottom line was that she had something he wanted—her time— and, since appealing to her professional ethics hadn't worked, because she apparently had none, then maybe the truth would.

"Three years ago," he blurted out, barely able to conceal his irritation at having to do so, "my sister disappeared. I was on an assignment in the United Kingdom when it happened, so I didn't find out until after I got back to the States, a couple of weeks later." He caught the door with the tips of his fingers before it collided with his foot and held it open. "By then, whatever leads the local police thought they had were cold and the world had pretty much moved on to the next tragic story. To everyone else, including the police, it's a cold case, but a body was never found and I believe that's because she's out there somewhere. So I still look for her."

His announcement was met with complete silence, during which time she didn't open the door again but she didn't close it, either. He chose to take that as a good sign.

"Hers is the other case that I'm working right now," Broderick went on. "Around the same time that I got the news that Meagan was on the run again, a new lead into my sister's disappearance popped up—the first one in over a year. I have some associates looking into it as we speak but if they find something significant, I plan to be the one who follows up. Since I can't be in two places at one time, that's where you come in."

He breathed an audible sigh of relief when the door slowly moved in reverse and she came into view again. "Plus," he added, catching her eyes and cocking a brow, "you'd be saving me from having to make a very difficult choice."

"What did you say your name was?"

"Broderick Cannon," another woman's voice said from somewhere behind the first one. His head snapped up and his gaze quickly roamed the foyer beyond the woman standing in front of him. By the time he had located his target and zeroed in on her, she was already walking toward them, moving up behind her identical twin slowly and eyeing him warily. "What are you doing here?"

"Talking with you, I thought." He slanted a chastising look in the other woman's direction and received a grin in return. He barely resisted the urge to grin back at her.

Well, that explains it, he thought as he stared into Elise Carrington's eyes and mentally commanded his swooning cock back into semihibernation. In a blatant act of rebellion, it yawned and stretched against his thigh, and then tightened in anticipation.

Right down to their facial expressions and physical mannerisms, the resemblance between the two women was beyond uncanny. As far as he could see, the key to the only identifiable difference between them rested squarely in his groin. The woman standing in front of him was just as beautiful as the one who'd just walked up, but he hadn't once caught himself wondering what she tasted like. His mouth was definitely watering now, though.

Elise—the *real* Elise—had traded her sexy dress and designer boots for a pink fleece jumpsuit that zipped up the front and bare feet. The material clung to her curves like a second skin, revealing just how dangerous to a man's sanity they really were. He couldn't help staring.

A throat cleared softly and he looked up to find two sets of amber-colored eyes trained on him—one wide and unblinking, and the other alert and amused. Not the least bit repentant, he cleared his own throat and tried again. "Miss Carrington, as I was just explaining to your sister, I'd like to talk with you about what happened between us earlier."

She cocked a brow. "Elise."

"I'm sorry?"

"I said, *I'm Elise.*" She touched a delicate hand to her chest in case he needed a visual. "You obviously can't tell me apart from my sister, so…"

They stared at each other, one of those *if looks could kill* stares, and he was the first to look away.

Okay, so she was pissed. He got that. But if she thought they were about to have a repeat of their interstate showdown, then she was sadly mistaken. For one thing, he was tired and starving, and for another, every synapse in his brain was on overload at the moment, blindsided by a swift punch of lust that had completely missed his gut and exploded, instead, in the center of his groin. He hated to ruin her diabolical little plan but divine intervention couldn't have helped him hold up his end of an argument just then.

"Okaaaay," Broderick hedged carefully. "I believe I'm completely clear now. So can we talk?"

Her other eyebrow joined the first one, high up on her forehead. "No."

"Elise—"

"Elise," her twin said at the same time. "You're being rude."

Elise turned to her sister with murder in her eyes. "Excuse me?"

"I'd like to hear what he has to say," the other woman murmured close to Elise's ear.

To Broderick, she said, "I'm Olivia Carrington." Then she extended a hand and shook his firmly. "I think you've already met my sister."

"That I have," Broderick confirmed, liking Olivia immediately. After a few seconds, he released her hand and turned his attention back to Elise. "That I have," he said again, his voice turning thoughtful.

"Well, then, welcome to Carrington Consulting. Come inside," Olivia said and took Elise with her as she moved aside so that he could do just that.

Chapter 5

Olivia was sprawled across Elise's king-size bed with her feet waving in the air, lying in wait for Elise when she emerged from her walk-in closet with a packed Louis Vuitton carryall and her portable gun safe. "That delicious specimen downstairs," she said, sitting up and announcing as soon as she spotted Elise, "is Broderick Malcolm Cannon." She consulted the iPad in her hand and nodded in approval at what she saw on the glowing screen. "He's thirty-seven, single and, according to the information that Eli was able to dig up on short notice, *very* financially solvent, which is always a plus in my book. Oh, and he owns Cannon Corp, which is apparently some sort of underground investigations firm with hush-hush assignments and a very high-level security clearance. Even Eli couldn't find out much about it,

but he did say that our Mr. Cannon has a reputation for
being a bit of a beast in the field, so we can assume that
he's probably at least a little dangerous." She paused to
giggle delightfully. "And, hopefully, an animal in bed,
which makes the fact that Eli didn't find anything to
support your theory that he could be a serial killer *very*
good news. For you, I mean." She set the iPad aside,
looking pleased with herself until she noticed Elise's
incredulous look. "What? I'm sorry but he's hot. Did
you really expect me not to comment on it? What is it
about fine men, exactly, that makes you so nervous?"

"I'm not nervous," Elise said, lying through her teeth.
She dropped her carryall on the upholstered bench at
the foot of her bed, then plopped down next to it and
unlocked the gun safe. Opening it, she took out a pearl-
handled Ruger .38 pistol and began loading it. "What
I am is pissed." When she was done, she snapped the
revolver into a leather holster and dropped it inside her
tote. "I can't believe I let the three of you talk me into
this." Badger was more like it but, whatever. Either way,
the result was the same—she'd been ganged up on and
guilted into hostile compliance. Adding an apologetic
and pleading Joel to the mix via Skype had not only
compounded the pressure that Olivia and Broderick had
piled on her, but it had also been a stroke of evil genius
on Olivia's part. She was good, Elise had to give her
that. Damn good. The traitor.

"Why can't you believe it?" Olivia asked, and Elise
didn't buy the confused expression on her face for one
second. "This is a perfect example of why you and I
started Carrington Consulting in the first place, isn't

it? To help people? *To help women?* If you'd stop thinking about yourself for one second and think about the
situation from Mr. Cannon's perspective, you'd see that
he's really nothing more than just another client who's
in need of our services."

"Let's not forget that he's just another client who,
according to Eli, runs a very successful security firm
of his own. If he handles the kinds of cases that you
and Eli seem to think he does, then he probably has re-
sources at his disposal that we've never even heard of.
Doesn't it seem a little strange to you that he needs my
help? Why doesn't he just put one of his minions on
Meagan's trail, so that he can deal with his other case
without any interruptions?"

"Probably because, thanks to the little fender bender
that you caused this afternoon, there isn't time."

"Of course there's time," Elise refuted, jumping up
from the bench and throwing up her hands in outrage.
When Olivia only smiled, she snatched up the safe and
took off for the closet again, unable to shake the feeling that she was being hoodwinked and bamboozled.
The more she thought about it, the more irritated she
became. "Meanwhile," she chirped in a voice that was
somewhere near the soprano range, "don't I get a say
about how I choose to spend *my* time?" She brought a
pair of jeans and a sweater out of the closet with her
and dropped them on the bed.

"Of course, you do," Olivia cooed.

"Except that, thanks to you and Mr. Chippendales
down there, apparently, I don't." She shrugged out of
her jumpsuit, tossed it on the bed and snatched up her

jeans. "He doesn't really need me and you know it. And stop calling him 'Mr. Cannon.' You're such a suck-up."

"Maybe so, but you have to admit that this arrangement makes sense. This way, if something does come up while you're together, it'll be easier and less time-consuming to deal with. Besides, it probably won't even come to that because, thanks to Meagan's obsession with social media, you already know that she's in the Jefferson City area and has been for several hours. Once you two get there, you could drive from one end of that place to the other in, what, an hour or less? You'll find her, toss her in the car with you and get back on the road," Olivia predicted, waving a dismissive hand. "Trust me, you'll be back here by this time tomorrow evening, if not before, at which time I will try very hard to refrain from saying 'I told you so.'"

Elise paused in the midst of jumping into her jeans to glare at Olivia. "All right, then why don't you go in my place?"

"I would, only I'm not the one he was down there seducing in his mind. You are."

Elise's sigh was long-suffering. "Why is everything about sex with you?" she asked, dropping a peach cable-knit sweater over her head and smoothing the hem around her denim-clad hips. "I think you need to see someone about that."

"I think it's cute that you think that," Olivia shot back. "The question is, why is nothing *ever* about sex with you? My God, Elise, loosen up a little, would you? He was flirting with you. He couldn't take his eyes off you just now and you didn't even seem to notice. How long has it been since you've been out on a date, because this could be a prime opportunity for you to—"

"Are you serious right now, Olivia?"

"Oh, come on. Tell me you don't find him attractive and I'll shut up."

Elise was instantly conflicted. Despite the fact that she and Olivia were opposites in more ways than they were alike, they couldn't be closer. Even when they were at each other's throats, they'd always been as thick as thieves, partners in crime in whatever nefarious scheme that one or the other had masterminded. If there were secrets between them, Elise couldn't think of very many, and, if there was a subject that was or had ever been off-limits, it didn't immediately come to mind. Under different circumstances, keeping the fact that she was attracted to a man from Olivia wouldn't even occur to her. It wasn't like she'd never been pursued by a man or been interested in one, and, contrary to what Olivia seemed to believe, she had actually dated twice as many men as she'd ever slept with. Which wasn't saying much, but, still. It was just easier for both of them if Olivia didn't know every single detail of her sex life. Like the fact that she'd just turned thirty-three and had only ever had three lovers. She knew her sister, and, in Olivia's hands, information like that would die a very slow and painful death.

Did she find Broderick Cannon attractive? Of course she did. What red-blooded woman in her right mind wouldn't? But that was another little nugget of information that Olivia didn't need to know because, with it, she'd have the power to drive Elise crazy.

"Okay, yes," Elise reluctantly conceded. "He's attractive. But that's not the point. This isn't a date." She snatched up a pair of silver hoops from her dressing table and put them on, then reached for her watch. "This is me being tricked into riding off into the night with a man that I barely know. Which reminds me, in the event that I'm never seen or heard from again, do me a favor and tell Mom and Dad that I did love them, no matter what you always said to them behind my back." Olivia was giggling way too hard for Elise's taste. "I'm glad you think I'm so amusing."

"Not amusing, just in dire need of some serious loosening up. You do know that we're not in high school anymore, right? There are no more midterms and finals to study for. It's okay to have a life now." She caught the distressed look on Elise's face in the dressing-table mirror and launched into a full-fledged laugh. "Hey, I'm just trying to save you from a future filled with a bunch of cats and a house that looks like a shoe."

"Yeah, well, as long as this shoe house of mine has a heated pool and local pizza delivery, I'm good." She stepped into tan pumps and grabbed her cell phone from the dressing table as soon as it rang.

"I'm just saying. No one would blame you if you let your hair down a little…for once. I can't think of a better way to kick off a vacation than with hot, sweaty sex. Milk isn't the only thing that does a body good, you know."

Relieved to see Eli Seamus's name flashing on her cell's screen, Elise touched an icon to accept the call and put the phone to her ear. She covered the mouthpiece, hissed at Olivia to shut up and, when she didn't, waved a hand for her to at least quiet down. "Eli," she said into the phone. "Hi, thanks for getting back to me so quickly. Please tell me you found something helpful."

Nearby, Olivia murmured something about seeing her downstairs. After nodding, she listened to what Eli had to say.

As soon as she'd been able to pry herself away from the dynamic duo downstairs, she had excused herself to her room to change clothes and pack an overnight bag. But first, she'd called Eli and shared what little case information there was with him, hoping that he'd be able to pin down Meagan's exact whereabouts quickly enough to eliminate the need for a partnership and, even worse, a road trip. But, as she listened to Eli's report, she realized that there was no way out, at least not yet, anyway. He agreed to stay on top of things and let her know if something interesting popped up but, in the meantime, it looked like she was stuck playing Robin to Broderick Cannon's Batman.

Dammit.

Resigned to her temporary fate, Elise emerged from her bedroom ten minutes later, ready to get the show on the road. She found Olivia and Broderick in the study, sitting close together, with their heads bent even closer and their voices hushed. "I'm ready if you are," she announced, interrupting their nearly nose-to-nose exchange. Their heads flew up guiltily, as if they'd been caught sharing government secrets. Trying not to scowl, Elise slung her tote strap over her shoulder and looked from one face to the other. She wasn't jealous.

Really, she wasn't. But, damn, did Olivia *ever* turn it off? "Shall we go?" she asked, glancing at her watch meaningfully and then pinning Broderick with another look. He rose from the couch slowly, smirking. *Was he really smirking?*

"Of course. After you."

"*Truth* or *dare*?"

She turned away from the passenger-side window and looked at him like she was surprised to see him sitting in the driver's seat. "What?"

"I said, *truth* or *dare*?"

It was almost ten o'clock at night, and they'd been driving in complete silence for an hour. A few miles back, at around the halfway point, the Hummer's GPS navigation system had routed them away from the interstate and onto an isolated stretch of paved service road that weaved through several miles of pitch-black farmland. It would eventually lead to a rural road in Jefferson County, and, shortly afterward, they would enter Jefferson City limits via a small residential community on the south end of town. But not for at least another three thousand six hundred seconds, which, in Broderick's estimation, was just about enough time for the spicy, exotic fragrance clinging to Elise's skin to finish driving him crazy.

Every time he inhaled, he was transported back in time to a mission in Bangkok, to a smoky massage den in the red-light district, and a 3:00 a.m. curfew that he'd taken his punishment for missing with a sleepy, satisfied smile. Every exhale was an irritating little reminder that it had been five months since he'd known anything close to that kind of satisfaction.

Something had to be done and, unfortunately, *Truth or Dare?* was the first PG-rated solution that came to mind. It wasn't the best idea that he'd ever come up with but a distraction was in order and at least this one would end the ridiculous silence between them. *Or not*, he thought as the light cast by the dashboard console illuminated the doubtful smirk on her face.

"I'm not playing a silly game with you, Mr. Cannon."

He bit down on a smirk of his own and cocked a brow. "Don't tell me you're afraid."

"No, I'm not afraid and I'm not ten, either, so your peer-pressure tactics won't work on me."

He glanced over at her and then took his eyes to the rearview mirror. "You sure about that?"

"Of course. Why wouldn't I be?"

"Then prove it," he challenged, catching her eyes for one tense second and then winking at her. "Play with me."

"No." Crossing her arms underneath her breasts, she shifted in her seat until her both her knees and her nose were pointed toward the passenger-side window. She looked like a proper nineteenth-century schoolmarm, except that he was 99 percent sure that she wasn't wearing any panties underneath her skintight jeans, and, if he stood over her at just the right angle, he could see down the front of her sweater. Her breasts were freckled, too, and bubbling out of the top of her bra in a way that was anything but proper.

"Come on, Elise," he cajoled playfully. "Help me out

here. I'm starting to feel a little restless and I could use a distraction right now. So play with me." He saw her hesitate and, sensing that he had the advantage, pressed a little harder. "Come on…you know you want to." She rolled her eyes at him and cracked a smile.

"All right, *fiiine*," she said, dragging the word out over four irritated syllables before ending on a hard *n*. "But I'm warning you, I'm never going to choose *dare*, so don't even waste your time going there."

"Fine," Broderick parroted, making her giggle. "Same rules here, though. If you aren't accepting dares, then neither am I. But," he added, putting up a finger to stall her when she opened her mouth to respond, "to compensate for the loss of *dare* privileges, I have to insist that all *truth* responses be completely and totally honest. No bullshitting to get out of giving straight answers allowed."

"Agreed." She shifted in her seat again. Pointing her knees in his direction this time, she crossed her legs, leaned into the armrest and propped her chin on her fist. "Let's go then," she said, bouncing a foot in the air. "I'll go first. You've probably already guessed by now but, just to be clear, I choose *truth*."

"*Truth* it is. Why don't we start with where you went to college and what your major was?"

"Gee, you're a real risk taker, aren't you?"

"See? You're already breaking the rules. Just answer the question, please."

"Whatever. I went to Northwestern and I majored in pre-law." He didn't miss the subtle sniff of superiority in her voice. Northwestern was a good school, a damn good school, and she knew it. "And I graduated in the top five percent of my class, in case that was your next question."

"It wasn't. How does someone who graduated from Northwestern in the top five percent of her class end up calling herself an investigations consultant instead of an attorney?"

"You make it sound like a step down."

"Isn't it?"

"No, it's not. I may not spend my days and nights huddled in muddy trenches, wallowing in my own filth and dodging land mines, like you, but my work is still very satisfying."

He wasn't the least bit offended. "So, you're saying that chasing around cheating husbands is more satisfying than taking them to the cleaners in a court of law?"

She caught him off guard with a deep, throaty laugh that put every nerve in his body on full alert. "You know, for someone who's supposed to be so smart—didn't I read somewhere that you graduated from high school when you were sixteen?—you seem awfully misinformed."

His eyebrows shot up. "You did a background check on me?"

She quirked a brow. "You *didn't* do one on me?"

After a second, he shrugged. "Yeah, I did. While you were packing, I did a quick check to see if you had a criminal background," Broderick admitted after a few seconds of holding her lovely gaze. "But, unfortunately, I couldn't dig up anything significant on Carrington Consulting in the short time that I had to look, and I was wondering if that was because there's nothing much to find."

"Hardly. Carrington Consulting caters to a very select clientele, so discretion is crucial to the success of most of the cases we take on. More often than not, they involve missing persons, high-profile circumstances and wealthy families who would prefer to keep their dirty laundry private, so broadcasting what we do and who we do it for is definitely not the objective. Sometimes we're able to make problems disappear without having to involve law enforcement, but situations like those tend to be the exception. As a general rule, we do what we do, and then we fade into the background and let law enforcement take all of the credit for it."

"Give me a 'for example.'"

"What?"

"I said, give me a 'for example.' It's just the two of us here. Your secrets are safe with me, so give me a 'for example.'"

"You want me to name a case that Carrington Consulting handled but that law enforcement took the credit for?" He nodded and she looked thoughtful. "Okay, um…the story out of Virginia, the one where the teenage girl wandered into a police station early one morning, after having been missing for several months. Do you recall that case?"

"Yeah, I do. She told police that she'd been kidnapped and forced into prostitution by a man she met online. She said that she was only able to escape after the house they were holed-up in was burglarized. The perps found her in a basement bedroom and let her go."

"There was a total of six underage girls being imprisoned in that house when Olivia and I sent our associates inside to contain the situation and retrieve the girl we'd been hired to find. She was the one they released. The other five were 'discovered'—" she paused to put up air quotes "—safe and sound by police when they raided the house a few minutes later, acting on an anonymous tip, of course."

"Of course. They found the two guys who ran the house bound and gagged in a utility closet." He slid her a look and chuckled. "Nice touch." They shared a smile. "Give me another 'for example.'" He liked the sound of her voice.

"The Michelson scandal."

"The guy who swindled people out of millions with insurance scams and disappeared," he said, nodding.

"That's the one. He's in prison now because of us."

"I'm impressed," Broderick said, meaning it. Michelson had almost managed to fall off the face of the earth. "I imagine it must be hard, living with never being able to take credit for your work."

Her gaze skipped away from his. "You'd be surprised at what people can live with, Mr. Cannon. Besides, we're paid very well for the services we provide and that's always a plus. Which brings me back to my point…"

"Which is?"

"That my time is much too valuable to waste chasing sex-starved men who can't keep it zipped up and consoling the heart-broken women who can't live without them. If you ask me, the society we live in is way too obsessed with sex. Thank God *I'm* not."

"Wow," Broderick ventured carefully as he leaned forward and pressed a button on the dashboard. "Back to the point, indeed. That was a passionate little speech you just gave. You must really hate sex." A built-in monitor lit up, displaying an interactive map of Jefferson City and its surrounding counties. Cannon Corp had attached an electronic shadow to Meagan's cell phone several hours ago and, right now, it was tracking her physical location and marking the geographical coordinates with a flashing red dot on the mobile computer screen. He was as relieved to see that her location hadn't changed as he was to learn that, as of an hour ago, she'd done them all a favor and stopped posting to her various social media accounts. No new posts meant no new embarrassing snapshots going viral and no new rambling, unintelligible status updates that would have to be explained away later. There were enough of those floating around already.

He toggled to a second screen to check for status updates on his other case. Seeing none, he dimmed the monitor and sat back. He had dispatched field agents to Albuquerque as soon as the lead had come in this morning to evaluate its validity and report back. That was over twelve hours ago. There should've been something to report by now. He'd sent two of his best men, and, in the back of his mind, he knew that if there was something to report, they would, but the waiting was starting to work his nerves. If there was any consolation to be had in the entire situation, it was the fact that had he followed his first instinct and gone after the lead himself, he would have missed the opportunity to encounter and eventually seduce Elise Carrington.

And that would've been a completely different kind of damn shame.

"How did you manage to get that from what I said? I've never had any problems with sex."

"But you think it's highly overrated."

"Isn't it?"

He thought about it for a second, then shook his head. "No, it's not and anyone who thinks that is insane."

"That's exactly what I'd expect a man to say. Whose turn is it now? Mine?"

"I think so."

The GPS system's automated narrator spoke up just then. *"In three hundred feet, turn right onto Highway J."* He switched on the turn signal and prepared to follow directions.

"I choose *truth*."

"All right, my question for you is, why are men so obsessed with sex?"

Broderick glanced over at her and took in the confused expression on her face before slowing to a stop, turning right onto Highway J and then merging with eastbound traffic. "I've known plenty of women who enjoy sex just as much as men do. Trust me, it's not just a male thing."

"Oh? Exactly how many women have you known, Mr. Cannon?"

He glanced at her again and collided with her steady, incriminating gaze. A chuckle rumbled in his throat.

One day soon they were going to break the nearest bed clean in two, he was convinced of it. But until then... "I'm sorry, is it your turn again, because I don't think it is?"

"It's not, but I'd still like an answer, please."

"I bet you would, Miss Carrington, but a gentleman never kisses and tells. Besides, it's no longer your turn, it's mine. *Truth* or *dare*?"

"You already know my choice."

"Okay, *truth*. How many lovers have you had?"

She gaped at him. He didn't miss the fact that her face was so flushed that it was practically glowing in the dark. "That's not fair! You can't refuse to answer a question and then ask me the same question and expect an answer."

"I can and I just did. Tell you what, why don't you take a few minutes to double-check your math while I find us a parking space?"

"Where are we going and why do we need to park when we get there?"

"We passed an all-night diner about a mile back," he explained as he exited the highway and turned onto the outer road that was parallel to it. "I thought we'd stop and eat."

"But what about Meagan?"

"She's probably already eaten by now. You, on the other hand, aren't much use to me if you're running on fumes." She turned a skeptical look on him and he shrugged. "What? Meagan hasn't left the area in hours and we're less than half an hour away from her right now. How much more damage can she do in the twenty minutes that it'll take us to refuel?" he asked, turning onto the parking lot and weaving through a line of idling transfer trucks. He found a parking space and shut off the engine.

"Recalculating your route," the automated narrator advised before it powered down with the rest of the vehicle.

"Based on what you've told me about her, a lot. I really don't think we should—"

"Look, I'm starving and it's not like I really need your permission to stop, is it, Sister Mary? Stop being such a goody-goody and come on. Let's eat."

She divided a look between his face and the nearly empty diner. Inside, a bored-looking waitress strolled the length of the counter to plop a plate that was piled high with French fries in front of a customer. He felt, rather than heard, her sigh of longing.

"All right," she finally agreed, albeit reluctantly. "We'll eat, but we have to be in and out of this place in fifteen minutes or less. I know you didn't graduate from Northwestern, like I did, but you *can* count that high, can't you?"

Silently Broderick took his pistol from a hidden dashboard compartment and snatched a cell phone from the dashboard cradle. Tucking them into hidden pockets, he caught Elise's eyes as he swung the driver's door open.

The look on her face was smug. Too smug. He hated to burst her little elitist bubble, but... Well, no, he didn't.

"I have an advanced degree in computer engineering from Brown University, Miss Carrington," he explained as humbly as possible. "I was writing code, building websites and hacking through firewalls in junior high school. So, yes, I can count that high." His stomach growled. "Now, are we done here? Because, if not, we're about to have a *very* interesting conversation about what's on the menu for dinner."

Chapter 6

An hour later, Elise was stuffed and her thoughts were racing. Thanks to their ongoing *Truth or Dare?* tournament, sharing a meal with Broderick hadn't only been only a surprisingly entertaining turn of events, but it had also been extremely enlightening. Without it, she'd never have discovered that, lurking just beneath his muscle-bound, powerhouse exterior was the soul of a technology geek—one who designed electronic firewalls for Fortune 500 companies by day and jumped out of helicopters, armed to the teeth and ready for whatever, in the black of night. She'd never have pegged him as one of those coffee fanatics who special ordered his coffee beans all the way from Cuba and ground them himself in a custom grinder, or as a closet Harry Potter fan, who'd read every book about the juvenile wizard *and* seen every one of the movies at least twice. And she certainly wouldn't have guessed that he could speak to her in French, simply asking her to pass the ketchup for his fries, and cause a spontaneous orgasm to explode at the very tip of her already-fretful clitoris. It had taken every ounce of self-control that Elise possessed to keep from stripping naked and begging him to do something illicit to her, right there on the booth's cracked Formica tabletop.

He was a study in contradictions. *Like Superman*, she mused as he paid the check and they filed past a line of incoming exhausted-looking truck drivers to the exit. Part bashful nerd and part sexy superhero, except that she was positive that he'd never been bashful a day in his life and Superman had never been so fine. Which was why, she suddenly decided, she was going to sleep with him.

Someday.

Maybe.

She took out her cell and checked for messages as they strolled across the gravel parking lot to the far end of the building, where the Hummer was parked. Unfortunately, there were none from Eli, but she'd missed a call and two separate back-to-back text messages from Olivia, just a few minutes ago. She glanced at her watch and frowned—it was almost midnight—then touched an icon on the screen to retrieve the texts. She regretted it instantly. Deeply.

It was just like Olivia to send obscene text messages across open frequencies, as a primary means of communication. Along with her latest visual transmission—

two extremely vivid images of a naked, embracing couple, locked together at the mouth *and* at the waist—came the declaration: *Just do it!*

"Uh-oh," Broderick said from just beyond her shoulder.

Startled out of the trance that the explicit images had put her in, Elise stopped short, pressed the phone to her chest and cringed. Had he seen Olivia's text over her shoulder? *Oh my God.* Of course he had, and now he was probably thinking that she was some kind of sex fiend.

Tossing her cell back inside her tote, she slowly turned to face Broderick. "Um, about what you just saw—" Whatever else she'd been about to say died in her throat when she saw that he was busy with his own cell phone. *Thank God.* Her relief was short-lived, though.

Broderick's gaze flickered up from his cell's screen to hers and a devilish smile toyed with his full lips. "I just got a text. You're not going to believe where Meagan is."

Her eyebrows joined his in the stratosphere. "I hope you're not about to tell me that she's not in Jefferson City, because I swear to God—"

"Oh, she's there, all right," he said, motioning for Elise to resume walking as he composed and sent a responding text. She did, and he fell in step behind her. "She's just in the last place that either of us would ever expect her to be." When he was done, he put away his cell and then reached around her to aim his key fob in the Hummer's direction. At the press of a button, the engine roared to life, the headlights switched on and the electronic locks released. The interactive dashboard was booting up when they climbed inside and fastened their seat belts.

"Recalculating your route," the automatic navigator advised as soon as Broderick shifted the Hummer into gear and drove off. They found their way back onto the highway in silence.

"Are you going to tell me where Meagan is, or do I have to guess?" Elise prodded when two or three minutes passed and no further explanation was forthcoming. The look he slid her made the hair on the back of her neck stand up. "What? Has something bad happened? Is she hurt?" The smile that curved his lips was reminiscent of the big, bad wolf. "Broderick..."

"Would you calm down?" he said, chuckling darkly. "Meagan is fine. She's just possibly...uh...*indisposed* at the moment."

"'Possibly indisposed'? What does that mean?"

"It means that right now she's at a place called *The Farm*."

Elise was lost. Was he playing some kind of silly word game with her? Really? Right now? "Okaaay. Well, where is this farm and what is she doing there? Riding bulls?"

"I know you're being facetious, but that could actually be the case."

Elise did a double take. "I'm sorry, what?"

"Calm down."

She hated being told to calm down, especially by a man. Broderick's overly calm, placating tone was irritating enough by itself, but playing cat and mouse on top of that was really pushing it. "Don't I look calm? Just tell me what's going on."

"I will, but first I have to warn you, Elise. What I'm about to tell you might—"

"You know, you're really starting to get on my nerves."

"You haven't had sex in almost two years. *That's* what's probably getting on your nerves."

Elise sat up in her seat and nailed Broderick with a murderous glare. "I knew I shouldn't have told you that!"

"Of course you shouldn't have because now I fully intend to use it against you every chance I get." The Hummer suddenly lurched forward, picking up speed rapidly and eating up the dark road beyond the windshield. "Look, I'll tell you what. I consider myself a decent person, and I wouldn't want to get on your nerves any more than I apparently already have, so why don't I just shut up and let you see for yourself where Meagan is?"

Her gaze wandered across the console and found his waiting patiently. "Fine," she bit out.

"Fine."

Oh, yeah. She was definitely going to sleep with him.

Maybe.

Someday.

If they didn't kill each other first.

"I could kill you!"

Rolling his eyes to the ceiling wearily, Broderick followed both the threat and the woman behind it inside the hotel room that she had insisted they get and closed the door at his back. If she was really going to kill him, he thought as he took in the neatly made double beds, fluffy-looking pillows and the flat-screen TV mounted to the opposite wall, he hoped she'd wait to make her move until after he had showered and was in a deep sleep. The place wasn't exactly the Ritz, nowhere near it, actually, but it was clean and the beds looked soft, which was a good thing because he was exhausted. Her suggestion that they stop to rest and regroup was a valid one. There wasn't much else they could do at the moment, anyway. The fact that the hotel was the only one for miles and there was only one vacancy, forcing them to share a room, was an unexpected but very pleasant bonus.

They'd been inside The Farm for over an hour and had searched the entire place twice before Broderick finally succeeded at prying information out of the stone-faced doorman, and even then there hadn't been much to learn. Yes, Meagan and her boyfriend were there earlier, but they'd left several hours before Broderick and Elise had arrived. According to the doorman, nothing remarkable had stood out about Meagan and her date, except that they were younger than most of the other patrons in attendance at the time. They had gone up to the second floor only briefly before leaving and Meagan had forgotten to retrieve her iPhone on her way out. Broderick had pocketed the phone, wondering what the hell Meagan was up to and hoping that she was at least being safe in the process. Even without the added burden of mental illness, two spoiled, privileged college kids, off on a spontaneous road trip, with plenty of money at their disposal and no sense of personal responsibility, was a train wreck just waiting to happen.

Bypassing Meagan's password and hacking into her cell phone was child's play. Sixty seconds after they climbed back into the Hummer and he pulled the device out of his pocket, he was scrolling through her contact list and reading her texts. It had taken him a little longer to plant a LoJack-style worm in her phone and shoot it through to her boyfriend's cell phone, but, even with Elise's husky voice buzzing nonstop in his ear and the intoxicating scent of her cologne damn near crossing his eyes, he managed to get through it. Now that they were trapped alone together in a hotel room, he'd be lucky to get through the next couple of hours.

Through a slit in the curtains at the window, he spotted an indoor pool and fantasized about dunking Elise a few times…in the deep end. Then he sighed and tossed his overnight bag on the bed. *Did the woman* ever *shut up?*

"I still can't believe I let you and Olivia talk me into this wild-goose chase," Elise railed, dropping her overnight bag on the bed closer to the bathroom and fighting her way out of her coat. She slammed it on the mattress, then sent her tote hurling after it. "Almost two hours we were in that place and for what, Broderick? What exactly did we accomplish?" She stepped out of her shoes and raked her fingers through her hair, those gorgeous amber-colored eyes of hers staring at him expectantly.

Broderick opened his mouth to respond, missed

his nanosecond-size window of opportunity, and then snapped it shut again. Poker-faced, he unfastened his watch and set it in on the desktop. His platinum cuff links clinked onto the wooden surface next.

"Oh, wait," she went on, tearing into her overnight bag mercilessly. "What am I saying? We did get two things accomplished. Let's see, first, we were able to successfully retrieve Meagan's iPhone from a new-age brothel, which, according to the doorman of said brothel, Meagan accidentally left there *several hours ago*." She had just about emptied the bag's contents onto the mattress when she finally unearthed a toothbrush and a tube of toothpaste, which she promptly brandished at him like a two-pronged weapon. Secretly amused, he eyed it and her warily as he shrugged out of his coat and strolled over to the closet with it.

What she needed, he decided in a sudden burst of mental clarity, was sex. But not just any sex, his tingling cock reminded him. She needed the kind of sex that would break the bed, send her drifting off into a peaceful, satisfied sleep, and then have her walking funny the morning after. And as he strolled back the way he'd come, he wondered if she had any idea just how close she was to getting it.

"And let's not forget," she continued, "that we can now report back to Joel and his wife, whom I'm sure are worried absolutely *sick* by now, that, while we have no idea where their underage daughter actually *is*, we do, however, still know exactly where she *isn't*." She paused to suck in a deep breath and release it slowly, looking genuinely troubled. "She's underage and on the loose with a reckless playboy who's old enough to get into adult sex clubs and also connected enough to take her with him. Did I miss anything?"

Several seconds of silence passed before he realized that she actually expected him to speak. And that was only after he glanced up from the desktop, where he'd been busy setting up a portable workstation, and ran right into her simmering gaze. "Don't you think you're overreacting just a little?" was all he could think to say.

"No, I don't." She folded her arms underneath her breasts and shifted her weight to one side, a brow cocked. "For all we know, Meagan could be across the border, somewhere in Mexico right now. What in the hell is she thinking? If I were eighteen and dating an older guy, who took me to a sex club, I'd—"

"You'd probably be somewhere right now with your bra up around your neck and your ankles around his," Broderick speculated jokingly. "Admit it, Elise. Carry on all you want but all that sex in the air turned you on and you know it. I saw the look on your face when we walked in on that three-way sixty-nine." She looked like a deer caught in headlights, making him snort with laughter. "It was hot. This is a safe place, Sister Mary. You can admit it."

She bristled and flushed at the same time. "All right, it was hot. A little...busy, but still hot." She noticed him vibrating with silent laughter. "What's so funny?"

"Nothing. I'm just having a hard time reconciling the image of the tough, no-nonsense cop that you say you were, with the inexperienced, damsel-in-distress vibe that you've got going on right now. It'd be funny if it wasn't so damn sexy."

"Stop flirting with me, Mr. Cannon."

"Tell you what, Miss Carrington. I'll stop flirting with you if you'll stop flirting with me."

"I'm not flirting with you." She seemed to remember the items in her hand and held them up as proof. "I was just going to brush my teeth. But, before I do, I would like to point out that just because I don't make a habit of doing something doesn't mean that I've never seen or heard of it. I'm not as innocent as you seem to think I am. I just happen to prefer quality over quantity. Is that a crime?"

The look he gave her was a cross between marriage and murder. He'd never known a more nerve-rattling woman. *Or a more exciting one.* "I believe it's possible to have both."

"That lady back at The Farm certainly was, wasn't she? Having both, I mean," she mused, setting aside her toiletries and folding her arms as she sauntered over to him. Walking into the V of his open legs, she studied the computer screen curiously. "What are you working on over here, Inspector Gadget, and how can I help?"

"Well, while you were busy working through a sudden onset of post-traumatic sex disorder, I was LoJacking Meagan's boyfriend's cell phone. Sit down, I'll show you." She surprised him by not objecting outright. "I don't bite," he murmured in her ear a few seconds later, as she settled her butt onto his lap and went along for the ride when he rolled them closer to the desk and pressed a button on the keyboard. It took every ounce of self-control that he possessed to ignore the weight of her butt in his lap and the feel of his hard cock pressing into its softness like a concrete speed bump. Settling a hand at her waist, he stifled a groan and told himself to focus.

"According to the map—" he began in a strangled voice, thinking that her cologne was the devil.

"Oh, goodie, the map," she chirped and clapped her hands together like a delighted child.

"You hate the map because you fear the map."

"I don't *fear* the map." He watched her roll her eyes to the ceiling and bit back a smile. Soon, he promised himself, he'd make her eyes roll for completely different reasons. "The map is just a map. What other handy little gadgets have you got in that bag of yours?"

"You probably wouldn't know what half of them were, even if I explained each one of them to you."

She reared back, pressing a palm against her chest like a true Southern belle, and stared at his profile with exaggerated offense. "I'm sorry, but was that a crack about my perceived lack of investigative skills?"

"Possibly." He sat back in the chair and gave her his full attention, challenging her with his eyes. "What if it was?"

"Oooh, someone's got jokes."

"Did you really think I was going to let that *Inspector Gadget* crack slide without a clap back? Come on now, Elise. You should know better than that by now."

A smile played with the corners of her mouth. "Touché. But while I do see your point, the fact remains that I take insults very seriously, especially when they're coming from someone who wants to sleep with me. It

occurs to me that this isn't the first time you've insinu-
ated that you're better at your job than I am at mine."
She sat back, too, and turned her head, bringing her
luscious mouth to within inches of his.

"I never said that and I don't believe that I've ever
said that I wanted to sleep with you."

"Oh?" She shifted on his lap, rolling her butt back
and forth across the granite pole underneath it slowly
as she held his gaze.

They stared at each other.

"Touché," Broderick finally said.

She tsked softly and shook her head. "Oh, ye of little
faith. Tell me, Broderick, you wouldn't happen to be
interested in a little professional wager between frenemies, would you?"

"Frenemies? That's an interesting way of putting
it. Go on."

"What if I said that even though *you* can't find your
sister and you're supposedly the best in the business, *I*
can? That's how good I am."

The laugh that Broderick had been doing his best to
suppress broke free before he could stop it from tum-
bling out of his mouth with a dark, cynical twist that
begged the question: *Are you out of your mind?* When
Elise failed to laugh with him, he sobered up by degrees,
looking at her like she was crazy. "You're serious."

"Yes, I am. I told you, I take insults very seriously.
So, what's it going to be? Are you in or are you out?"

He looked up from watching her lips move and caught
her eyes. "Suppose I was in, what are the stakes?"

"If I win, I want the Hummer."

"Damn, that was quick. Would this be the same Hummer that you've previously referred to as a rolling monstrosity?"

She dimpled at him and he had a sudden urge to feast. "Let's just say that it's grown on me. Don't tell me you're afraid you'll lose?"

Don't sweat it, Broderick. She won't win, anyway. "Not at all." *But you will.* He scraped the skin beneath his bottom lip with his teeth for a second as he silently weighed his options. She had issued him a dare, so there was really only one way to properly respond, wasn't there? "Fine. The Hummer. What do I get if I win?"

"That depends. What do you want?"

"You," he said simply and just as quickly. "With your fine ass. I want *you*. And since the Hummer is on the table and she happens to be very special to me, I'm going to have to insist on an entire night with you— any way I want you and as many times as I want you. Are you up for that, because you know you're going to lose, right?"

Elise's face and neck were beet red when she cleared her throat and sucked in a shaky breath. "Fine. If you win, *which you won't*, then yes, I am up for that. I'll have to be, won't I?"

"All right, then I'm in." This was going to be like taking candy from a baby.

"You won't be saying that when I'm selling off your precious Hummer, piece by piece, for parts."

Chapter 7

The water was sparkling and clear, it was the middle of the night and Broderick was the only one enjoying it. Glancing at the sign posted on the far wall, advising guests that both the pool and the hot tub had closed for the night hours ago, he tugged off his T-shirt, dropped it at his feet and dove into the deep end in one fluid motion.

The plan was to swim laps until he no longer had the energy to think about how tempted he was to slip his hand between Elise's thighs and wake her from her nap with an orgasm. Then and only then could he return to their hotel room and continue with the pretense of being even a little bit civilized. As it was, every time she slanted her feline eyes in his direction and hurled some smart-ass, thinly veiled insult at him, he was tempted to give her something else to do with those glittering, suckable lips of hers besides sniping and snarling.

Something nasty.

At the shallow end, he kicked off from the wall and started back the way he'd come, hoping that the bracing water cleared his head and checked his raging libido. It wasn't like him to let a woman get so deeply under his skin, especially one who was moody and talked too much, and never while he was on an assignment. Rounding up Meagan and delivering her back home to her parents didn't necessarily fit that description, but it was still a time-sensitive task—one that he needed to wrap up as quickly as possible, so he could focus on the latest development in his sister's disappearance. There was no telling when he'd have free time like this again and it wasn't like leads on the case were constantly pouring in.

Any paper trail that Brandy Cannon might've left behind had dried up shortly after her disappearance and so had any viable leads. Three years later, tips into her disappearance were so few and far between that getting laid should've been the last thing on Broderick's mind now that a new one had finally popped up. He had busted up human sex-trafficking cells all over the globe and brought countless women and girls home to families who feared they were lost forever. Smuggled hostages out of hostile foreign territories and strolled onto hundreds of playgrounds, two steps behind absentee parents who had stolen their children and relocated halfway across the world with them. But none of his specialized training or years of field experience was doing a damn thing to help him find the only family he had left.

The last time they had seen each other was at the reception right after his parents' funeral, where, rather than mingle with the other grieving attendees, they'd spent most of the time holed up in the kitchen of their parents' house, arguing about the man Brandy intended to marry. Broderick had taken one look at Dennis Dortch and pegged him for the oily businessman that he was, but she was completely under the man's spell. Possibly he'd said some things to her that he shouldn't have and wished he could take back, and possibly she had, too. But they hadn't sworn each other off completely.

Kicking off from the wall again, Broderick reminded himself once again that it was just a matter of time before he found Brandy. There wasn't a rock that she could hide under that he couldn't find and overturn. He just hadn't yet stumbled upon the right rock. *Yet.*

Which was why he needed to be focused on finding the rock, not toting one around in his boxers. He got to his feet in the shallow end, swiping water out of his eyes and willing the rock that was currently trapped inside his shorts to cease and desist.

"You know the pool's closed, right?" Elise's voice broke the silence abruptly, forcing him to quickly shift mental gears. Just like that, he was off course again and careening toward a conscious wet dream.

"If that's true, then you aren't supposed to be here, either. So why are you, Miss Carrington?" He turned his head slowly to the left and found Elise standing at the edge of the pool in her bare feet. She'd showered earlier and changed into black, knee-length leggings and a blue T-shirt before lying across one of the beds for a power nap. Now she looked rumpled and well rested, ready for round two. "Are you here to pick up where we left off fighting earlier or to start a new fight altogether?"

She surprised him by dropping into a seat at the edge of the pool and lowering her calves into the water. "Neither. This time, I come in peace. The water looked tempting, so I thought I'd join you, that's all." Her feet drew circles below the surface.

Broderick could think of a few things that looked even more tempting to him, but he kept his mouth closed. Thoughts of Elise had followed him into the shower, turning him into *that* guy—one who stood underneath the spray for a ridiculously long time, stroking his straining erection like a horny teenager and fantasizing about her. He had cum twice before running out of hot water and finally getting out, and his cock was still dangling between his thighs in the chilly water like a lead weight. So, yeah, keeping his opinions to himself was definitely his best bet.

"In a few hours, it'll be dawn," he said. "You should still be asleep."

She slipped into the water with him like an eel. "I just woke up and I'm wide-awake now." He watched her swim a circle around him and then pop up out of the water less than a foot away from him, swiping water out of her face. He took one look at her dripping hair, at the droplets of water clinging to her eyelashes, at her see-through T-shirt, which was now molded to her unencumbered breasts, and his throat went dry. Her nipples jutted from her full breasts boldly, topping the jiggly globes like ripe blackberries. His mouth watered.

They were the most beautiful things he'd ever seen.

"Elise…" Chuckling incredulously, he massaged a wrinkle out of his forehead with tense fingers and prayed for patience. Was she trying to kill him? "If this is your idea of revenge for offending you earlier, it isn't very nice." She reached up and swept her hair back from her face. The action caused her breasts to sway from side to side hypnotically.

His nostrils flared.

"Revenge would've been walking in, in the middle of your 'shower,'" she said, putting up air quotes and cocking a brow suggestively. Broderick howled with laughter. Blushing to the roots of her hair, she looked down at the water and cracked a smile, then back up at him for the briefest of seconds before her gaze skated away and her face burst into flames. "Believe me, this isn't that," she said quietly.

Broderick tipped his head to one side and searched her eyes. "What is it, then?"

Her cheeks burned, but she didn't look away from his penetrating stare. She wanted him to see what she was thinking, to see all of the things that she couldn't bring herself to say aloud. To put them both out of their misery and seduce her. Wondering if she was aware that *she'd* been seducing *him* ever since he'd first laid eyes on her, he reached out and slowly filled his hands with her butt cheeks. Her eyes widened when he began drawing her closer to him and she gasped when he snatched her up out of the water. Face-to-face and chest-to-chest, she wound her arms around his neck and pressed a whisper-soft kiss to his lips. That was his first clue into what was going on in that mysterious mind of hers. His second was the soft glide of her tongue across the seam of his lips and the throaty moan that tumbled out of her mouth when he ground his cock into the V of her thighs.

She quivered from head to toe when he pushed his hands inside the back of her pants and gripped bare skin. Silent complicity. But he still needed to hear her say the words. "Cat got your tongue?"

"I don't know what this is." He swallowed her gasp. "I've been thinking about it, and I can't figure it out. We're at each other's throats most of the time. We can barely stand each other, so..."

"Why do we want to screw each other's brains out?" he finished, dipping his tongue into her mouth and toying with hers lazily.

"Exactly. It doesn't make sense, does it?"

"Does it have to?"

"Shouldn't it?"

"Not necessarily." He held her eyes as his fingers wandered into the secret valley between her thighs from behind and underneath. Her eyes slid closed, and she bucked against him. He parked his lips next to her ear. "Chances are that, after this case is closed, we'll never see each other again. It'll be like we never met."

"Like time that never happened," Elise agreed breathlessly. "Untime. Except that we'll both know—"

"That it did. Imagine how many times I could make you cum between now and then. In *untime*."

"I *have* been imagining it." He rewarded her tortured-sounding honesty with a soft kiss on the lips. "I can't *stop* imagining it. That's why I came out here—" She sucked in a sharp breath. His fingers were on the move. "T-to extend an olive b-branch."

"You came out here to call a truce?"

"It's the professional thing to do, don't you think?" The pads of his fingers glanced across her clit and she started violently. "Oh, God, this is s-so unprofessional," she panted next to his ear. "But it feels so...g-good."

Licking his way past Elise's parted lips, Broderick buried his tongue so deeply in her mouth that it was a wonder she didn't choke. His tongue lapped against hers in perfect sync with his adventurous fingers, skillfully manipulating her flesh until an orgasm was humming in her throat and her slack mouth could no longer participate in the kiss. She wilted against him, resting the tip of her nose onto the bridge of his and staring at him through a cross-eyed haze of lust. Seeing but not really seeing. He was close to cumming himself, just watching her.

"This is untime, remember?" His lips found the shell of her ear and the tip of his tongue flickered against it suggestively. "A time that really isn't time, when both nothing and everything is exactly as it seems, and there's no such thing as rules...or professionalism. In untime we make love, not war."

"I s-suppose we could always go back to f-fighting... later."

"We could...later. Any suggestions for what we might do in the meantime?"

She dipped her head and tongued his neck softly,

almost shyly. Tasting him as if she was satisfying a long-held curiosity. Licking him like his flavor was her favorite thing in the entire world. He drew in a shaky breath and released it a moment later, buried in a throaty, helpless moan. The clock was ticking on what little restraint he had left. "Elise…"

Her moist lips were suddenly at his ear. "I thought maybe that we could start counting…in untime."

"I see." Without warning, Broderick hiked Elise up in his arms, banded an arm around her waist and cupped her sex with his free hand. "Why didn't you just say so?" The pads of his fingers swam around in her juices, finding her clit and working it frantically as her startled cries grew louder and louder, and she rode the friction like a jockey. "One," he growled into the valley between her bouncing breasts as he sank one long finger into the midst of her pulsing walls and triggered an explosion.

Elise didn't recognize herself or the sounds coming out of her mouth. She didn't know how to process the hot licks of pleasure heating every inch of her skin from the inside out. In some distant corner of her mind, she heard the crudely uttered gasps, high-pitched shrieks and breathless pants lighting the air nonstop, and saw herself spread out on the bed underneath Broderick's powerful body, bucking and writhing uncontrollably, and cringed at the helpless picture she made.

She wanted to run her fingers along the hard muscles in Broderick's arms, fill her hands with the smooth, brown skin on his broad chest and touch her fingertips to the deep ridges in his chiseled abdomen. She wanted to be wide-eyed and alert for the moment that he finally peeled off his swim trunks and she saw him completely naked for the first time. But every muscle in her body was suspended in anticipation, waiting with bated breath to see where his hands and mouth would land next, what they would do when they got there and how delicious it would feel. Weightless with arousal, she grabbed a handful of the bedsheet on either side of her and watched him through slitted eyes.

Done feasting on her mouth and neck for the moment, his head descended and his long pink tongue darted out from between his lips to lap at one puckered nipple. As if it were dripping honey, he sucked at it delicately, hungrily, drawing it deeply into his mouth to dance with his tongue, and then biting at it lightly with his teeth. Every nip, flicker and tug from his masterful mouth set off a corresponding pull in her groin that nearly brought tears of delight to her eyes.

Her hips bucked off the mattress and then began rocking in time with his lapping tongue. "Oooh, that feels so good." Her mouth fell open and her eyes slid shut.

"You like that?" he murmured between licks.

"Oh, God, *yeeees.*"

"So do I," he said, as he turned his head to pay equal homage to the other nipple.

Elise had never seen anything like the mesmerized look in his eyes when he tossed her on the bed and stripped off her leggings and then whipped her dripping T-shirt over her head and sent it flying. She'd never before witnessed the rapturous look on his face as he stretched her mouth wide for his tongue and kissed the breath out of her. She felt sexy and alive. Powerful.

Broderick wanted her; she'd always known that. He hadn't exactly made a secret of it. But why had no one ever told her what it felt like to want just as badly as you were wanted?

His fingers combed through the small patch of heart-shaped hair at the apex of her thighs and she trembled. Instantly craving more, Elise welcomed his mouth when it sought hers again and opened her legs even wider for his searching fingers. "Look how wet you are," he growled against her lips, his fingers gliding into the slick folds down below and swimming around leisurely in her warm honey. Her breath caught in her throat and she writhed on the mattress. A frustrated cry shot out of her mouth when his fingers just barely missed colliding with her pulsing clitoris once again.

"Please," Elise begged when the pressure between her thighs had built to a feverish level.

"Please, what, Elise?" he murmured soothingly against her neck. "This?" he asked, slowly sinking one long finger into her tight heat and stroking her rhythmically. She shrieked and he chuckled wickedly. "Or this?" He wanted to know, as he trapped her pulsing clitoris beneath the pad of his thumb and worked it slowly, deliciously, until she wilted into the mattress and orgasmed so hard that she blacked out. "Aww," he crooned as he slanted his mouth over hers. "That's a good girl. That's right, cum for me, baby."

That was the last thing Elise heard before his tongue

invaded her mouth and sucked her up into another diz-
zying kiss.

"Open your eyes, Sleeping Beauty."

She did, slowly and languidly, feeling as if she was
waking from a deep and satisfying sleep. Finding Broderick hovering over her, she reached out and touched him
for the first time since leaving the pool, and hummed
with satisfaction. His skin felt like velvet-covered steel
underneath her roaming hands. She skimmed her fingertips along the length of his torso and giggled like a
femme fatale when he shuddered violently, traced the
elaborate SEAL Trident tattoo on his right forearm with
the tips of her fingers and felt the sheer power of him
vibrating underneath his warm skin. "Feels like someone could use a cold shower," she teased, staring up at
him through the mess of her lashes.

"Not quite," he drawled before protecting himself
then coming fully on top of her and bracing himself on
his elbows on either side of her head. "But let me show
you what I do need," he said as his hips surged forward
and stretched the entrance to her throbbing canal in
a shocking instant that popped her eyes and snatched
her breath.

Faces less than an inch apart, they stared at each
other.

"Am I hurting you?"

"N-no." The breath Elise had been holding trickled
out of her mouth in short, choppy huffs as she shook
her head. *Hurting her?* My God, the man was huge,
stretching her wider than she'd dreamed possible. It
was all she could do not to let her eyes roll to the back

of her head in sheer bliss. "Y-you feel s-so good." He sank a little more deeply inside her and gritted his teeth, trembling with the effort to restrain himself. "So…oh, God…so g-good."

Just when she thought that she'd taken as much of him as she could, he slid his large hands underneath her and palmed her butt cheeks, tilting her hips upward and surprising her with one last, mind-numbing thrust. Elise swore she could feel him in her belly.

Broderick's self-control was slipping away by degrees, replaced by the overpowering need to plunder and possess. A sigh that was part defeat and part surrender whistled out of his mouth when Elise's walls collapsed around him from tip to base, and then his eyes crossed in his head. He was seeing two of her when he caught her hands in his, took them up and over her head and anchored them to the mattress.

"You're so tight," he hissed in her ear. "Like a virgin," he confessed as his hips began to move and she began to sing off-key to the rhythm they set.

Before long, his hips were dancing against Elise's erratically, wildly, with a mind of their own, seeking access to her silky heat from any and every angle possible. It seemed as if he couldn't stroke her deeply enough or quickly enough to satisfy the insatiable hunger building inside him. When the headboard started tapping against the wall behind it and her cries grew alarmingly loud, he told himself to pull back and pace himself. But the deeper he plunged, the more her walls quickened and pulsed around him, the tighter she closed around him like a slippery velvet fist, milking him mercilessly.

He wanted to prolong the experience, to make her cum a fourth and fifth time before finally seeking his own release, but she was electric beneath him. Her heels dug into the small of his back, spurring on his strokes, and, after he freed her hands, her nails dug into his shoulder blades hard enough to make him grit his teeth. He found her G-spot and stroked it again and again and again, and she began chanting, "Yes…yes… yes…" breathlessly in his ear. She greedily tongued his neck and shoulders until he could no longer fight himself. Defeated, he reared back, pressed his contorted face into her pillowy breasts and roared like a fallen Viking warrior.

Chapter 8

His cell phone was vibrating. Or maybe *he* was. *Still.* Every muscle in his body groaned in protest as he slowly lifted his head from Elise's chest and searched what he could see of the rumpled bed around them, looking for his phone. Making love with Elise had completely drained him, putting him right back at square one—in a state of sheer exhaustion. He had cum so hard that the muscles in his arms had damn near liquified and his heart was still racing. And now his cell was ringing and he had to move in order to answer it. *Shit.* If it hadn't been for the fact that they were supposed to be working, he would've let the damn thing wear itself out.

Half-asleep, Elise started when his weight shifted on top of her, but she didn't open her eyes. Purring like a kitten, she rolled onto her side and blindly reached for a pillow. Taking pity on her, he handed her one as he unfolded himself into a sitting position on the far side of the bed and put his cell to his ear. "Cannon," he said, trying his damnedest to focus on the voice buzzing in his ear, instead of the bobbing of his cock. Turning his back to the enticing scene on the bed, he scrubbed a hand over his face and forced himself to tune in. "Where?" he asked, silently bidding farewell to the idea of crawling back into bed with Elise and waking her up with his tongue in her mouth and his fingers between her thighs. Tamping down his irritation, he listened for several more seconds before walking over to the desk and hitting a button on the laptop's keyboard. The screen lit up, displaying a real-time map. "There's a commercial landing strip about a half-hour's drive north of here," he said into the phone. "Looks like it's part of an old dairy farm outside Columbia. Lock in my location and find it based on that, and then get landing clearance."

"What's happening?"

"Something's come up. We have to go," he said, turning just in time to catch Elise rolling out of bed and stretching like a cat. His knees went weak. "Give me an hour, then send the chopper. I'll meet you there," he said into the phone. "In the meantime, call me back if anything changes." He ended the call and tossed the phone on the bed, catching Elise's eyes. "The agents that I sent to Albuquerque this morning found a woman there who recognized Brandy's picture and claims she knew her. I need to go there now and speak with her personally."

Elise looked stunned for a moment, then she reached

for the bedsheet and tugged it free from the mattress. "Of course. I won't be long in the shower," she said, holding the sheet in place with one white-knuckled fist and scratching a nervous hand through her wild hair. She took in his naked body from head to toe, pausing a second or two to eye his cock curiously, and blushed to the roots of her hair. He grinned when her eyes started dancing around the room. "I'll…uh… I'll save you some hot water."

Now that she was fully awake and aware, the Elise that Broderick was frequently tempted to shake until her teeth chattered was back. Shoulders tense, mouth tight and holding on to the sheet for dear life, she slowly side-stepped her way around the bed behind her and headed for the bathroom, snatching a robe from the closet as she went. *Was it wrong to find her obvious discomfort sexy?* He watched her damn near skip the rest of the way to the bathroom, unaware that his feet had started moving in her direction until he heard himself say "No need" and saw her eyes widen with the realization that he was coming for her. *Again.* "Why don't I join you?" She hesitated for a moment, then dropped the sheet and disappeared into the bathroom.

He paused long enough to discard the battle-weary condom still clinging to his swollen cock and grab a new one from the grooming case that he'd left on the bathroom vanity. Then he stepped into the walk-in shower behind Elise and got right to work helping her soap herself from head to toe. Setting the condom on a built-in shelf, he filled his hands with shower gel from the pump underneath the shower head and took them straight to her breasts, massaging them gently as he tongued the side of her neck. He nipped at the balls of her shoulders lightly, wondering if this was what the beginnings of drug addiction felt like.

"You have beautiful breasts," he panted in her ear, meaning every word. Her nipples peaked under his flickering fingertips and her head lolled to one side, baring even more skin to his seeking mouth. He licked and sucked at it greedily as he ground his straining erection into the valley between her round butt cheeks and teased her nipples until they sat atop her breasts like cherries. The breathless sighs, pants and moans that she gifted him with raised goose bumps on his skin and quickened his breath.

Broderick waited until she had pushed her ass back against him for the umpteenth time, silently inviting him to paradise, before giving his hand permission to abandon her jiggling breasts for the slick divide between her thighs. One, two, three strokes against her swollen clitoris and her entire body spasmed with an orgasm that seized up her muscles and stole her breath. Chuckling under his breath, he reached for the condom, tore open the gold packet and quickly sheathed himself. Filling his hands with more shower gel, he bent Elise over at the waist, gently soaped her back as she flattened her hands against the shower wall and braced himself as he slowly slid inside her from behind.

Her walls began pulsing around him immediately, bending his self-control into something that he no longer recognized. He watched himself sliding in and out of Elise's gushing tunnel and gave in to the savage growl rumbling in his chest. It bounced off the walls in surround sound as, over and over again, he surged into her so deeply that the force of his strokes lifted her heels from the shower floor.

Somewhere, beneath the sound of his own heartbeat roaring in his ears, beneath the sensation of a violent orgasm licking at the base of his spine, he heard Elise's high-pitched squeals, the sound of their wet flesh slapping against each other and her breathless promise of arrival, and let it push him over the edge into paradise.

The water was ice-cold when they finally got out of the shower.

"So...should we talk about it?"

The question, carefully posed in Broderick's deep, thoughtful-sounding voice, cracked the tension inside the Hummer like a whip, startling Elise out of a scandalous private reverie that warmed her skin with guilty embarrassment. She closed her eyes, cleared her mind of her prurient thoughts, and opened them again on the neat little farmhouses, weathered barns and grazing cows flying past her window. When had they gotten off the interstate?

Suddenly overheated, she cracked her window and inhaled the frigid air streaming inside the cabin gratefully, willing herself to get it together. She'd been reliving the experience of making love with Broderick over and over in her mind, recalling the grip of his strong hands on her butt cheeks and the ecstasy of bouncing back and forth on his long, thick shaft until her throat was raw from screaming her pleasure. As a result, right this very second, her nipples were puckered and tight, and the friction between the sensitive tips and her bra's lace cups was maddening. She could barely think straight, let alone string together a coherent sentence, so talking about it was out of the question.

"If by *it* you mean what just happened between us back at the hotel, then no, I don't think we should."

"Elise, you haven't said a word since we checked out of the hotel an hour ago, and we both know that isn't like you, so I think maybe we should. Obviously, you're upset—"

If only it was that simple, she thought and stifled a tortured groan. "I'm not upset."

"I don't believe you."

"I don't care," she volleyed back, her voice saccharine. "Could we please just drop it?"

"Whatever you say."

"Thank you." She flopped back in her seat and took a slow, deep breath. Her jeans were tight. Too tight, especially in the crotch.

They rounded a curve in the two-lane road they were following and nearly rear-ended an ancient-looking tractor that was suddenly directly in front of them. Cursing under his breath, Broderick slammed on the brakes and then swerved over into the oncoming traffic lane to avoid a collision. Luckily, there was no other traffic on the road. Once he'd sped past the charming old relic and the elderly farmer who was perched atop it in the driver's seat, bundled up against the elements, he noticed the chastising look on Elise's face and her death grip on her arm rests. He cocked a brow. "What?"

"Nothing. It's just…" Elise pursed her lips and studied her manicure. "*Someone* sure is in a bad mood today."

"Well, if by *someone* you mean me, then you just might be right." He consulted the directions to the landing strip one last time, then closed his laptop and slid it into a recessed compartment in the console. "I've been sitting over here for sixty very long minutes, with a beast of an erection resting in my lap and visions of your bouncing breasts dancing before my eyes. That goddamn cologne of yours, which, I'm sorry, might as well be a schedule-one narcotic, is seriously starting to mess with my head and to make matters worse, I can't seem to recall a time in my life when my cock has ever been as hard as it is right this minute. So, yeah, I guess I am in a bad mood this morning. But you said you didn't want to talk about that, so…" He trailed off, shrugging helplessly.

"I don't suppose it has occurred to you that I might be having a bad morning, too?"

"Why would it? I seem to recall suggesting that you might be upset just few minutes ago, and you said you weren't."

"That's because I'm not. I'm just…processing everything."

"You've never had a fling before." It wasn't a question.

"How could you tell?"

"For starters, you blush like a virgin every time I look at you," he said, flicking a glance in her direction just in time to see her do just that. "And then there's the fact that you were tight enough to cross my eyes."

Determined not to let him see how much he was arousing her, Elise looked away.

"Would you want to have a fling, Elise?"

Elise's head whipped around and her eyes widened. "I've n-never really given it much thought."

"Oh. Okay. Well, perhaps while I'm away, you will."

"Perhaps," she agreed quietly.

"Good," he said, just as something beyond the windshield caught his attention. He directed her attention toward it with a nod. "The landing strip that we're looking for belongs to a local dairy farm that's been closed for years. It's just over this next hill." They summited the hill in question and he pointed through the windshield at a dark spot hovering in the sky a few miles off in the distance. "There's my ride. Do we need to go over the plan again?"

Impressed with the sheer size of the helicopter circling in the air up ahead, Elise sat up in her seat and eyed the machine through the windshield the same way that she would've eyed a gorgeous pair of Louboutin's. "No, but I would like to review the terms of our bet again. Is it too late to choose a different gadget as my prize?"

"Yes, and, if it makes you feel any better, my chopper would never have been on the table in the first place. As it is, the Hummer will only be in your possession for a few short hours, so don't bother going to the trouble of adjusting any of the settings or getting too comfortable in the driver's seat." He noticed her lingering gaze through the windshield and shook his head, chuckling. "Trust me, she'll never love you the way she loves me, so stop drooling and pay attention, please. The plan. Are we clear on it?"

Elise reluctantly took her eyes off the shiny black machine slowly descending to the ground up ahead. "Yes, but I don't know if I like the idea of crashing through the front door and dragging Meagan out by the collar." Because of his abrupt departure, they weren't going after Meagan until later that night, when, according to Broderick's intel, she'd be with Peter Danforth at an off-campus frat party. Until then, Elise was going to stay behind in Columbia, babysit the Bat Mobile and continue electronically monitoring their activities until he returned.

"Why not? It could be fun."

"That's true but it could also be dangerous, Broderick. This is the Midwest and Columbia, Missouri, isn't exactly known for its racial harmony. I say we get in and out as discreetly as possible."

"All right. How do you suggest we do that?"

"I'm not sure yet, but I'll think of something before you get back. Worst-case scenario, I'll just kick in a window and dive through it." She noticed the look on his face and did a double take. "What?"

"I'm trying to imagine you diving through a window in a miniskirt and stilettos."

"Trust me, it can be done."

"I believe you, but do me a favor and hold off on breaking and entering until after I get back. I don't want to have to come back here and bail you out of jail. By now one of my men has already been in contact with Danforth, so he knows we're coming for Meagan and he knows what I expect him to do when we get there." He pointed to the compartment in the dash where the laptop was stored. "I'm still tracking his cell and monitoring his communications, so if he's stupid enough to make a suspicious call or send a text that's in any way suspect, the system should alert you immediately. If or when something happens, we'll figure out our next move then. What about the computer software? Any questions?"

"Did you remember to jot down the log-in information like I asked you to?"

He nodded. "Yes, I left a note on your iPad."

"Then, no, no questions."

"What are you going to do with yourself while I'm gone?"

"First, I plan to find the most expensive restaurant in town and sit down to a nice breakfast. Then, I don't know, maybe I'll go to confession. I've been a very bad girl." She meant it as a joke but there wasn't a trace of humor in his eyes when they met hers across the center console.

"Oh, yeah? Are you Catholic?"

Elise grinned. "No."

"Then you might as well take this to confession with you," he said, reaching out and hauling her across the console to meet his tongue halfway.

"Are you out of your mind?"

Elise took her cell phone away from her ear long

enough to shrug into a plush white robe. She folded the soft material closed around her naked body and knotted the belt around her waist. "Considering everything that's happened in the last twenty-four hours, I think that's pretty much a foregone conclusion," she said, putting the phone back to her ear and stepping into the matching slippers that had been set out for her. She accepted a champagne flute filled with cranberry mimosa—her second one—and smiled her thanks to the hovering attendant. Incredibly relaxed after an hour-long Swedish massage, she sipped at the sweet, frothy liquid delicately as she followed the attendant out of a candlelit massage room and down a long corridor. "I slept with a man that I barely know and I enjoyed every minute of it. What does that tell you?" she murmured into her cell as she walked.

"It tells me that I had it wrong all along. You're not a robot." Olivia's throaty chuckle drifted through the phone. "Didn't I tell you it would be good, that *he* would be good? I have a sixth sense for these kinds of things, which reminds me. While you're there, do yourself a favor and get a Brazilian wax. He looks like the type who'll appreciate the gesture appropriately."

"I'm sorry, but that's the last thing I plan on getting while I'm here."

"Why?"

"Because it hurts like hell and I'm already sore in places that I completely forgot about. I'm not brave enough to take on any more pain right now."

Armed with the keys to Broderick's Batmobile, Carrington Consulting's Black Card and a host of sore muscles that were screaming for some tender, loving care, Elise had driven the Hummer the five-mile distance from the landing strip to the city limits of Columbia, Missouri, and checked into a suite at the Hilton. After unpacking, sending her clothes out for dry cleaning and eating a light room-service breakfast, she'd been planning to shower and then crawl into the king-size bed for a much-needed nap.

But then the concierge arrived with the extra towels that she'd requested at check-in and a complimentary gift basket from a local day spa, and she'd been struck with sudden inspiration. After what she'd been through during the past twenty-four hours, she figured it wouldn't hurt to take some time out for a little pampering. She justified her indulgence by bringing along her iPad and working on the closing notes for her last case in between, and, when possible, while she was being serviced. It was a win-win situation, but a mani-pedi and a Swedish massage was about as adventurous as she planned to get.

A Brazilian wax? Uh, no.

Her next stop was a stark white, private bath room that was flooded with natural light and tastefully decorated with a variety of lush, exotic-looking potted plants. There, she turned over her robe once again to the attendant, put away her iPad and activated the speakerphone function on her cell. Setting it and her glass on a nearby ledge, she slipped into a tub of warm, bubbling Italian mud up to her neck, gazed up at the sky through the huge skylight centered over the tub and sighed with contentment.

"What's a little pain in exchange for all of the pleasure you'll receive?"

"Whatever. If I recall correctly, the last time I got a Brazilian wax, I was tempted to call the police afterward and report that my poor flower had been assaulted by a bearded John Wayne Gacy look-alike." Olivia howled with laughter. "Not to mention the fact that the guy that I was seeing at the time definitely did not know how to appreciate the gesture appropriately." She paused to think for a second. "Quincy! That was his name. Do you remember him?" Another whoop of laughter burst through the phone, making Elise giggle, too. "He was like a Hoover vacuum down there. I couldn't cross my legs for a week after him." She sipped her mimosa and waited patiently for Olivia to finish laughing and catch her breath. Several seconds passed before she did.

"All the more reason you should take full advantage of your current situation. I mean, think about it, Elise. How often does a woman find herself alone, on a road trip with a gorgeous stranger who's good in bed *and* not a complete lunatic?"

Elise couldn't help laughing at the idiotic question.

"You see?" Olivia queried, laughing, too. "It doesn't happen very often, and, honestly, it couldn't have happened to a more deserving person."

Elise's smile vanished. "Just what is that supposed to mean?"

"It means that you're over thirty and you've barely scratched the surface of the Kama Sutra. It means that there are more than two sexual positions in the known universe."

Elise frowned at the phone. "I know that."

"Good, now go forth and try out some of them. Broderick Cannon is the perfect excuse to let yourself go, for once in your life. I say, pick up an economy pack of condoms, take the long way home and explore your inner freak along the way. I want all the juicy details when you get home."

"I'm supposed to be working, remember? Which reminds me, I was dead serious about the question I asked."

"Oh, okay, well, then I have to ask you again—are you out of your mind?"

"Not at all. All I need you to do is quietly look into Broderick's sister's disappearance. Her maiden name is Brandy Cannon. I'll text you the rest of the information that I have on her shortly."

"I thought you said you were going on hiatus after you were done with this case?"

"I was. I mean, I am. Technically, this isn't really a new case. It's more like payback," Elise explained as she stared up at the skylights and watched the wind whip through the trees overhead. "Broderick Cannon might be great in bed but outside of it, he needs to be taken down a few pegs. I bet him that I could find his missing sister before he does."

"What? Isn't he in Albuquerque right now, looking for her?"

"Yes, but—"

"The man owns one of the country's top security

firms, Elise. If he hasn't been able to find his sister, what makes you think you'll be able to? What were you thinking?"

"I was thinking about how he somehow got it into that inflated head of his that all I do every day is chase down cheating husbands and shop for shoes. As if Carrington Consulting is a joke. I think I just wanted to shut him up."

"Well, he's kind of right about the shoe shopping part, but—"

"Really, Olivia?"

"Yes, really. Anyway, who cares what he thinks? The only real difference between what he does and what we do is that he's free to shout his accomplishments from the rooftops and we aren't. But we knew that would be the case when we started the firm, and, until now, neither of us has ever had a problem with it. What's changed?"

"Nothing's changed. You're right," Elise admitted, though it cost her dearly. "I wasn't thinking. I know I shouldn't care what he thinks, but he's just so damn smug that it makes me crazy."

Broderick's automatic assumption that she was some spoiled, airheaded, wanna-be private investigator stung, and it couldn't have been further from the truth. Her service record, both as a police officer and as a marshal, was impeccable, and, contrary to what he seemed to think, her decision to resign from the first had nothing to do with the dress code restrictions. She was good at her job because God knew she'd taken enough flack from men who thought the same way that Broderick did for the right to do it. And while, ultimately, she hadn't been content to make a career out of it, she'd spent more than enough time secretly eyeing her captain's office and mentally rearranging the furniture to her liking, up to that point. Then she had arrested a woman named Gloria Williamson and everything, including the way she looked at the law, changed.

"So what?" Olivia challenged, breaking into Elise's thoughts. "Look, I'm all for you having great sex, because God knows you need it. But don't forget for one second who you're sleeping with. Broderick Cannon is hot, I'll give you that, but I don't need someone with his level of security clearance poking around in my professional affairs, and neither do you, my friend."

"It doesn't have to get that intense. It's not like we're dealing with the IRS."

"Yeah, well, if given the choice, I'd much rather have the IRS snooping around than Broderick Cannon. Think about it, Elise."

The fact that Olivia, of all people, had to talk her out of doing something reckless went against everything that Elise stood for, both as an intellectual and as a feminist. It also spoke volumes about the current state of her personal affairs. When had she become one of those women who lost the ability to think clearly because of good sex?

"I will," she promised, sort of meaning it.

"Good. In the meantime, I guess it wouldn't hurt to put out a few feelers and see if anything comes up."

"I knew you loved me," Elise said, grinning from ear to ear.

"Oh, shut up. You owe me big-time for this."

"No, I don't. You're the reason I'm here in the first place, remember?"

"Hmmm" was the only sound Olivia made before the line went dead.

Gloria Williamson didn't cross Elise's mind again until lunchtime, when she was at the food court in the local mall, eating a Mexican lunch and people watching from a tiny table in a corner by the exit doors. Once or twice while she ate, her gaze landed on a woman whom she'd never seen before but who, because of some small gesture or facial expression, reminded her of Gloria and the thousands, maybe millions, of other women out there just like her. Quiet, soft-spoken women who tried not to draw attention to themselves and who apologized profusely whenever they did; women who, for whatever reason, tied themselves to destructive partners and then resigned themselves to their fates, suffering in silence. Once you knew what to look for, they were easy to spot and they were everywhere, hiding in plain sight, many of them masters of disguise.

Like Gloria Williamson.

The first time they had encountered each other outside the battered women's shelter where Elise had volunteered throughout high school and beyond, and where Gloria had been a resident on more than one occasion during that time, was at a department-wide Christmas party during Elise's second and last year as a police officer. They recognized each other immediately, their gazes meeting and locking for one alarming second and then darting away in different directions, hers nervous and Elise's stunned.

Over the years, she had frequently run into women on the street who'd been to the shelter, and she'd always pretended not to see them—the doctor who'd taken out her tonsils when she was sixteen, one of the science teachers from her high school, one of her mother's closest friends, the mother of one of hers and Olivia's closest girlfriends… the list was endless. But encountering Gloria was different because, as it turned out, she was the police commissioner's wife.

After that night, the next time Elise saw Gloria was on the evening news.

While the press was busy speculating on the hows and whys of Gloria's foiled murder-for-hire plot against her husband—Was she mentally ill? A black widow? Had there been some kind of secret love triangle going on that had spiraled out of control?—Elise took the news of the woman's ensuing fifteen-year prison sentence personally, like a blow to the gut. So much so that she quietly submitted her resignation a few months later and never looked back.

Did she regret it? *No.* Had walking away from a career in law enforcement and eventually starting her own investigations firm been as much of a step down from practicing law in a court of blind justice, as Broderick seemed to think it was? *Absolutely not.* Just thinking about the absurdity of that notion made Elise's blood boil all over again. Not being able to straighten him out about his ridiculous misconceptions was turning out to be a major exercise in self-control.

You know the rules, Elise, a little voice in the back of her mind piped up.

"Yeah, yeah, yeah," she grumbled under her breath. "I know the rules." By the time she finished at the spa and made her way back to the hotel, she'd gone over them a hundred times in her head.

"I'm sorry, miss, did you say something?"

She looked up from digging around in her tote and ran right into the front desk clerk's quixotic, blue-eyed gaze. The teen—her name tag identified her as *Jessica*—was wondering if Elise was a fruit cake, but trying to be polite about it. Elise recognized the look instantly and couldn't help smiling. She'd probably been walking around, talking to herself for hours, a sure sign that she was seriously sleep deprived. "I was just wondering if there were any messages for me while I was out," she said. "Carrington. Room 430."

"Just a moment, let me check, Miss Carrington." Jessica stepped away and was back a moment later. "No messages."

"Thank you." As if on cue, Elise's cell vibrated in her pocket. She took it out and read the text that had just come through as she made her way to the elevator. It was from Broderick.

Possible that I may need to be here a little longer than I anticipated. A couple of hours or so, at the most. Worst-case scenario, we meet at the frat house. Call you later with more details or if something else changes. Questions? Call me. In the mood for phone sex? Call me. Otherwise, get some rest.

Elise stepped onto the elevator and texted back: Will check out the frat house. Then rest.

Be safe, he replied.

You, too.

Back in her suite, Elise set up the mobile workstation on the desktop and logged in to the interface on Broderick's laptop. She checked up on Meagan and Danforth as she stripped down to her camisole and panties, and then, satisfied that everyone was exactly where they were supposed to be, toggled to another screen. A few seconds later, she sat down at the desk and went on a virtual tour of the frat house's interior and its grounds.

Afterward, she spent some time on her iPad, finishing up the notes for her last case and electronically submitting them to Carrington Consulting's online database. Then she climbed into bed, snuggled into the covers and set the alarm on her cell.

Chapter 9

Broderick approached the basement door of the Nu Theta frat house and tapped softly on the glass at after ten o'clock that night. A few seconds later, the knob turned from the inside and the door cracked. He pushed it open wide enough to slip inside and closed it at his back, quickly scanning the dim, mostly empty space beyond them over Elise's head before lowering his questioning gaze to hers. "How'd you get in here?"

She shrugged. "I picked the lock. How else?"

Except for the narrow glow from a single lamp that was sitting on a table at the far end of the basement, it was dark. A floor above them, rock music was blasting and bass was thumping, the bump and drag of overhead foot traffic was constant, and it sounded like everyone was talking at once and competing with one another to be heard over the music. But the air in the basement was still with inactivity. A beat-up washer and dryer was set up close to the steps leading to the main level, and that was apparently as far as anyone ever bothered to venture. The rest of the space was bare and dusty with neglect.

"Sorry I'm late," he said, tugging off his gloves and pushing them into the pockets of his down-filled vest. "The interview lasted a little longer than I expected and then, since I was already in the air, I stopped off at my place in Arizona to change clothes and pack more suitable clothes. Then I dropped by Cannon Corp headquarters for a briefing on a new case that I've been asked to take on after I'm finished here. Oh, and somewhere in there, I remembered to eat something before I passed out. Does anyone else know you're here?"

"Not that I know of. The backyard was clear when I picked the lock at the back gate and came in, and I disarmed the alarm system before picking the lock on the basement door, which—" she threw up her hands and quickly added when Broderick's eyebrows shot up "—I plan to fix before we leave, so calm down. What was I supposed to do, ring the doorbell? Besides, I've only been here a few minutes myself, and, judging from the questionable breeze that keeps wafting down here through the vents, I don't think anyone up there really cares about what's happening down here."

"Great. So Meagan is up there right now, doing God knows what, while my *partner* is down here, hiding in the basement and getting contact buzzed every few seconds. This just keeps getting better and better," Broderick joked as he took out his cell phone and followed her deeper into the basement.

"You're kidding, right? They're not even smoking the good stuff, so the most I have right now is a budding headache. Who are you calling, the police?"

"No, I'm texting Danforth to let him know that I'm here now and I expect him to make an appearance." He glanced up from the phone and did a double take, noticing her all-black getup for the first time and grinning to keep from pouncing on her.

She looked like a much sexier version of Catwoman, in her snug-fitting black corduroy jeans, matching sweater and stiletto boots. Her sandy-brown hair was swept back from her face and tamed into a glossy cap of liquid brass that brushed the collar of her fur-trimmed, black leather jacket. Together with her dramatic eye makeup and bold red lipstick, the outfit gave her a dangerous edge that was incredibly appealing, especially since, underneath all of the gloss and sex appeal, she wasn't really a cat at all, but more like a kitten.

She saw him staring and became suspicious. "What's wrong? Why are you looking at me like that?"

"No reason," he lied and took his eyes back to his cell to finish texting. He pressed Send, tucked the phone back in his pocket and took slow steps in her direction. "It's just… You look great and you smell even better. I was just wondering if—"

"Oh, no you don't," Elise warned, taking a step backward. "Don't try to distract me right now, Broderick.

I've been waiting all day to hear—" He reached out and hooked a finger into the waistband of her jeans, using the leverage to bring both her and her stiletto boots skipping toward him. She landed against his chest with a soft *oomph* of surprise.

"Why do you smell so damn good?" he dipped his head and whispered in her ear. His nose rode the slope of her neck lightly, inhaling deeply. "You smell like you taste…incredible." Groaning in appreciation, he slipped his arms around her waist, pulled her in even closer and pressed a soft kiss to the spot just behind her ear. "Did you miss me?"

"Don't flatter yourself," she said, pushing against his chest. Rearing back in the circle of his arms, she caught his eyes. "Stop trying to distract me. What happened at the interview? Did you find out anything helpful?"

"Not in the least." He hesitated for a second, then thought, *what the hell*. It never hurt to get a second professional opinion. "Let me show you something anyway." Motioning for her to move closer to the lamp's glow with him, he released her and took a thin stack of snapshots out of an inside pocket. He walked up behind her near the lamp, handed them to her and looked at the images with her over her shoulder. "This is the woman I met with today," he said, pointing out the woman in question. "Her name is Lynn Collins, and, according to her, the last time she saw Brandy was about a year ago, when they both lived in the same apartment building in downtown Albuquerque. If that's true, then Brandy was calling herself Sabrina Dreyfus at the time, and she looked like this." He touched a finger to one of two other women in the snapshot and waited for Elise's reaction.

"This woman looks nothing like the pictures of your sister that you showed me this morning." As if there was a possibility that she was seeing things and needed to double-check herself, she moved even closer to the lamp and leaned in. Just as he'd done earlier, she studied the woman in question intently, no doubt mentally comparing her short, spiky black hairdo to Brandy's shoulder-length brown hair; the prominent gap between her front teeth to Brandy's braces-perfect smile; and the extra twenty pounds that sat on the woman's frame to Brandy's boyishly thin frame. After several seconds of careful deliberation, she shuffled through the stack, studying each of the three additional snapshots just as intently. "I'm not seeing it. How could this Lynn Collins person have seriously thought there was a connection when, clearly, there is none?"

"I wondered the same thing," Broderick said, taking one last snapshot from his pocket and handing it over. "Then she showed me this."

Elise took the picture and stared at it, the expression on her face speaking volumes.

"You see it, too?"

"Yes," she finally admitted, flicking a startled glance up at him. "There's a little more of a resemblance in this shot. Around the mouth, I think…and the eyes. It's…" She kept staring. "I can't quite put my finger on it, but I feel like there's something I'm missing." Turning to face him, she gave him back the pictures and leaned back against the table behind her. "What are you going to do now?"

"Doing nothing at all makes the most sense. The chances of this woman and my sister being one and the same are virtually nonexistent. Supposedly, everyone has a twin out there somewhere. Obviously this Lynn Collins woman met what she thought was Brandy's twin. She was so convinced that I almost hated to tell her she was mistaken. Then I thought about the time I was wasting there, while you were here, alone, and I wanted to strangle her."

Elise blushed to the roots of her hair. "Thank you... I think. But the situation still sucks."

"Yeah, it does," he agreed, appreciating her. "My only consolation was the look on her face when she realized that she wouldn't be getting the reward money."

"Reward money?" Elise asked, perking up visibly. "Wait just a second. How much reward money are we talking about?"

"A hundred grand at last count." Broderick's gaze lowered to her red lips and lingered. "Not that you have a snowball's chance in hell of collecting it yourself. You can certainly dream, but I do believe pigs will fly first."

Her tone was soft and thoughtful sounding when she said, "You know...it's going to be so much fun remembering you said that when I'm putting your precious Batmobile on the auction block."

"So you keep saying."

"We'll see," she said brightly, dimpling adorably.

"But don't worry your pretty little head about that right now. You've suffered enough disappointment for one day. If it makes you feel any better, I was lying before, when I said I didn't miss you. I did…a little…sort of."

He moved closer and loomed over her. "Oooh, that does make me feel better."

"Good." She folded her arms and sat up to lean into his strength, holding his gaze even though her face was flaming and her nipples were tight. "Because I've been thinking about the question you asked me earlier—you know, the one about flings—and I bought condoms today while I was out. Just in case."

Down boy, Broderick mentally commanded his cock.

Thanks to the music pounding nonstop over their heads, they weren't in any danger of being busted for trespassing. *But,* he thought as images of himself with his pants down around his ankles and Elise's panties in his mouth flashed before his eyes, *in another two minutes or so they sure as hell would be.* Disappointment over the day's events had been pricking at his nerves for hours. He was wired up and his system was humming with wild, unchecked adrenaline, every ounce of which was currently focused on one thing and one thing only—burying himself inside of Elise's slick, tight walls as quickly as possible and cumming hard and fast. If he got his hands on her right now, she was liable to scream until her throat was raw and bring half the town running.

Envisioning it, a dark, almost sinister, chuckle slipped out of his mouth before he could check it. When

she took one last step toward him, he gave himself permission to pounce, snatching her up so fast that her eyes
flew open and her breath caught in her throat. She was
crushed against his chest, her head lolling to one side
when his mouth found her ear and the tip of his tongue
traced its shell delicately. "That's interesting. Guess
what I did today?"

"What?"

"I bought condoms…just in case."

Down boy, Broderick warned himself again in one
breath. In the next, she turned her head and came for his
mouth, and his tongue was plunging between her lips
hungrily. He wasn't aware that he'd moved until suddenly there was a dusty wall at Elise's back, her legs
were wrapped around his waist and he was grinding his
granite-hard erection into the V of her thighs, straining to get as close as possible despite the cloth barriers
between them. The kiss was wild and rough, wet and
full of teeth, lips and tongue. Deep and punishing, he
mused, momentarily withdrawing to catch his breath
and then diving in again. Just the way he liked it.

Neither of them was aware that they had company
until the sound of a throat clearing nearby slipped into
the midst of their dueling tongues and snapped them
both to attention. From the waist up, they sprang apart,
staring at each other.

Was that you? Broderick's gaze silently queried
Elise.

No, I thought it was you! her eyes shouted back at him.
In unison, their heads slowly turned toward the

source of the noise—a tall, willowy girl with stunning blue eyes and a shy smile. "Uncle Rick?"

Behind her, a Captain America look-alike was staring at them with unabashed curiosity.

Broderick glowered at him first.

"You must be Danforth," he snarled in lieu of a greeting. "Your timing sucks."

It was raining lightly when Elise and Broderick marched Meagan out of the frat-house basement and across the back lawn to the gate a half hour later. After quickly bundling her into the backseat of the Hummer, they hopped in out of the light shower themselves. Sullen and mutinously silent, Meagan huddled in a corner of the backseat, shivering in a thin denim jacket and flannel leggings and glaring out the window.

"I believe this belongs to you," Broderick said, producing Meagan's lost cell phone from a dashboard cubby and passing it back to her over his shoulder. She grabbed it and immediately tested its power, sighing with relief when the screen lit up and then frantically working the touch screen.

"Oh my God! I thought I lost my phone," she said. "Where did you find it? The last time I saw it was at the—"

"Sex club," Broderick supplied balefully. "Yes, we know." He glanced at her in the rearview mirror and shook his head. "I took the liberty of charging it for you, so now you can use it to call your parents and tell them that you're safe and on your way home."

"Why? They're just going to yell and I can wait until I see them for that. Besides," she whined in a voice that was almost pitiful sounding. Almost. "I've got a killer headache and I'm starving."

Elise and Broderick traded looks as the engine roared to life and he peeled off down the alley.

"Call them."

"Come on, Uncle Rick. I'll be home in, what, a couple of hours? If you're not going to feed me, the least you can do is let me sleep off my buzz before I see or talk to them. It's the only humane thing to do."

Broderick's sigh was long-suffering times ten. "Meagan... Elizabeth... Barclay," he growled, aiming a death look at her in the rearview mirror.

"Oh, all right, Uncle Rick, jeez! I'll call them, but could I please just have a minute to prepare myself first?"

"This isn't your first time pulling a stunt like this, Meggie. You know the drill."

"You used to be my favorite godfather. What happened?"

"You turned thirteen and discovered lip gloss, Spanish Fly and gangsta rap, that's what happened. And, as far as I know, I'm your only godfather, so lucky me. What the hell were you thinking? Any number of things could've happened to you, particularly in your condition."

"Wow, it sure didn't take long for you to bring that up, did it?"

"You had to know it wouldn't, given the seriousness

of the situation, Meggie. You aren't exactly known for making the greatest decisions under the best of circumstances. I don't understand how you thought that gallivanting across the countryside with some playboy jock, while you were in the middle of a manic episode and refusing treatment, was a smart thing to do."

"*Really*, Uncle Rick?" Sitting up, Meagan stuck her head in the space between the front seats and divided an incriminating look between Broderick and Elise. *"Really?"*

"You know, emphasizing a word to death in no way increases its power."

"Well, neither does ignoring the irony of the situation. *Which is*," Meagan emphasized, "the fact that you're lecturing me about good decision making and I just caught the two of you going at it in a frat-house basement. As a matter of fact, I think your fly might still be undone."

"No, what's ironic is that you *allegedly* caught me being a grown-ass man, while you were high as a kite and clearly under the influence of alcohol, both of which, at your age, are illegal substances."

Meagan's rebuttal was lightning quick. "I would like to point out that I was *allegedly* under the influence of illegal substances. You don't know that for sure, and I have admitted to nothing."

"Why don't you save your twisted closing arguments for your father?"

The Hummer merged onto the interstate and bullied its way over into the fast lane. Grumbling under her breath, Meagan flopped back against the seat and filled the cabin with the most tortured-sounding groan that Elise had ever heard. "This is so unfair. There are millions of teenagers in the world, and I have to be the only one who never gets away with anything. It's like I live in a prison or something."

"With a heated pool and a seasonal clothing allowance," Broderick reminded her. "Don't forget about the heated pool and seasonal clothing allowance."

"I beg your pardon, but a clothing allowance is a necessity, Uncle Rick."

"Sure it is."

Tongue-in-cheek, Elise looked up from the text that she was busy composing and darted a cautious glance at Broderick. Seeing that he was stone-faced with rage, she bit back a smile and finished her text. "I just texted Joel and Olivia with an update," she said, slipping into the exchange quietly. "They're aware that we're on our way home with Meagan."

"Thank you," Broderick said.

"You're welcome."

"Soooo…what's up with you two? Are you, like, a couple or what?"

"Or what," Elise and Broderick replied in unison, shooting each other surprised glances.

"You answered that pretty quickly," he murmured, glancing at Elise as he typed his password into the laptop and then tapped the glowing screen to summon a map. It popped up a second later, already in progress.

"So did you, now leave me alone." As entertaining as

his and Meagan's quirky little family dynamic was to watch and listen to, she was way too distracted to take an active role in it. The most she was capable of doing right now was appreciating Meagan's quick tongue and Broderick's obvious frustration from a safe distance, as evidenced by her attempt at invisibility throughout much of the play-by-play. She was in no shape for a fight, not with a hot, wet vagina pulsing between her thighs and a clitoris that was swollen to twice its size nestled within in its slick folds. Honestly, she was relieved that they'd found Meagan safe and sound, but if Broderick thought that Peter Danforth's timing was bad, then Meagan's was even worse.

Not only did Elise *not* relish the idea of an overnight road trip in weather that could create icy road conditions at any time, but she especially didn't like the idea of suffering through what was turning out to be an ongoing pre-orgasmic state with an audience on hand to witness it. Fighting with Broderick right now was a twisted sort of foreplay that she didn't need. Hadn't she been caught in enough compromising situations for one day?

If they hadn't been interrupted, she'd have had sex with him in a stranger's dusty basement, up against the wall like a horny teenager, with one of her breasts shoved into his mouth and her panties dangling from one of her ankles. And she would've loved every second of it. Coming to grips with that was titillating enough, because she'd never done anything like it before, but even more so was the sudden realization that she was pissed at the missed opportunity.

"I wasn't going to start a fight."

Her cell phone vibrated in her lap. "Good," Elise replied, reading the incoming text message. "Joel just texted back to let us know that they're waiting up and, apparently, Broderick, he's having their housekeeper prepare your favorite meal."

"Wait, so, not only do I have to listen to them yell and scream when I get home, but I have to eat eggplant Parmesan, too? Oh my…" Meagan threw up her hands. "This is unreal!"

"It sucks to be you, doesn't it?" Broderick asked the rearview mirror. His goddaughter's spoiled face pouted back at him. "Text him back, please, Elise, and tell him thank you, but we won't be escorting Meggie home tonight. I'm sending her by chopper, with two of my field agents, so she should be home in an hour and a half. I have some business that I need to finish up here."

"Why don't I have Olivia follow up with a phone call in the meantime?" Elise suggested as she began texting back. "In case they have questions that they'd like answered sooner rather than later."

"Wait, you're worried about me being alone with a college guy but you're sending me off alone, in the middle of the night, with two mysterious hunks who probably haven't seen a woman in God knows how long?" Meagan blurted out incredulously. "Should I be worried?"

"I'm sending you home with Agent Morris and Agent Stross. Remember them?"

"The gay guy whose wedding I sang at last summer and the Russian woman who used to be the head of Dad's security detail?"

"That would be them."

"Oh my God! You're killing me here, Uncle Rick! I mean it, I'm dead back here. Like, I'm actually about to flatline."

Grinning, Broderick glanced up at the rearview mirror. "Meggie?"

Meagan sighed. "What?"

"Shut up."

Chapter 10

"It's official. You're never going to be her favorite god-father again," Elise yelled at Broderick over the noise of the helicopter's spinning rotor blades. "You know that, right?" Smiling, she looked at him and found that he was already looking at her.

"She'll get over it," he yelled back at her, smiling, too.

Having just finished escorting Meagan to the Cannon Corp helicopter and handing her over to two of the most tight-faced, no-nonsense agents that Elise had ever seen—in person *or* on film—they were standing a safe distance away from the wind force of the blades, awaiting the chopper's takeoff. Behind them, across a swatch of wet grass, the Hummer was parked at the side of the road, with its headlights on, set to high beam and slanted in their direction for visibility. After the helicopter's landing skids lifted off from the landing strip, slowly rising into the night sky and taking its flashing lights with it, the path that the Hummer's narrow halogen beams illuminated for them was the only thing standing between them and pitch blackness.

Slanting a hand over her eyes against the gently falling rain, Elise watched the helicopter's ascent until its shiny black paint could no longer be distinguished from the night sky, then lowered her gaze to Broderick's face. His expression was blank and unreadable. She hoped hers was, too.

"So...we're alone again," he mused, still smiling.

Elise felt her face heating up, but she refused to look away. "So we are." *Am I really going to do this? Again?* "What's next on the agenda?" To have something to do, someplace else to look, other than into his sleepy-looking, mesmerizing eyes, she glanced back at the Hummer and then up at the dripping sky. "You mentioned unfinished business. Does that mean we're stopping off someplace else first before we go home?"

"Why don't we get out of the rain and talk about it?" he suggested, motioning for her to precede him to the Hummer. When she did, he fell in step behind her.

"All right, but if you've masterminded some kind of criminal plan that you think I'm going to participate in, then—" In the rural night air, the high-pitched chirping sound that suddenly cracked the silence was like a bomb going off. Elise jumped, then froze, looking around wildly. "What in *the hell* was that?"

Behind her, Broderick's deep, seductive chuckle

reached her ears a second before the Hummer's head-lights switched off and every thing went completely black. Unable to see her hand in front of her face, Elise stood still, waiting. "Broderick… I swear to God, if this is some kind of joke, I—oh my God!" He grabbed her around her waist from behind, pulling her back against him with splayed hands that instantly set off crawling in opposite directions along her torso. She was so distracted by the sensation of his warm breath shooting down the side of her neck and the tip of his dancing tongue against the shell of her ear that his X-rated intentions didn't fully register until she felt the front clasp of her bra pop loose and the arctic sting of cold air against her exposed skin. With the front of her jacket hanging open, the hem of her sweater bunched up underneath her chin and her naked breasts bouncing freely in the frigid air, she had no choice but to go along for the ride as he walked them closer to the Hummer.

"The only plan I've masterminded is one that involves making you cum in as many positions as I can conceive of before we both pass out from exhaustion," Broderick whispered directly into Elise's ear as he palmed her breasts and toyed with the tips of her nipples. She gasped when he licked the slope of her neck like it was a dripping ice-cream cone and then moaned when his teeth sank into the flesh there with just enough bite to make her shiver. "But, in case it matters, some of the things that I plan to do to you are still illegal in a couple of different states. Like this," he growled as they slowed to a stop and one hand left her jiggling breasts. Streaking down to the snap of her jeans, it quickly went

to work there. "I'm pretty sure that this is illegal...
somewhere."

Before Elise knew what was happening, Broderick's
hand plunged down the front of her jeans and cupped
her mound through her thong. "Your thong is soaked,
Elise," he accused as his fingers parted her slick folds
and dove in. "Oooh, and, look, so is your pussy."

Collapsing back against him, Elise's stomach hol-
lowed out in surprised delight. "Oooh," she moaned,
trembling as her hips began pistoning back and forth
against his long fingers with a mind of their own. He
sank his thumb and two fingers between her lips and
used them to expertly antagonize her clitoris, working the swollen nub like it was a joystick and he was a
master controller. Elise's toes curled inside her boots.
"Oooh, that feels s-so good...don't stop..."

He chuckled in her ear. "Do you have any idea how
hard my cock is for you right now, Elise?"

She bucked back against his groin, felt his thick erection pressing against her butt and released a long, shaky,
pre-orgasmic breath. "N-no."

"Would you like to find out?" Her knees nearly buckled when they started walking again.

How was she supposed to walk when every nerve in
her body was on fire?

"Oh, no you don't," he said, trapping her against him
with what felt like a steel band around her waist, while
his fingers continued their sensual assault. "Stay with
me, gorgeous. We're almost there."

She shook her head frantically against his chest. *"I
c-can't. Oh... I'm cumming! Oh, God... I'm cumming!"*

"What's the matter, Elise?" Broderick crooned in her ear. "We're only a few steps away from the Batmobile. Can't you wait?"

His fingers were playing so wildly between her thighs, swimming around in her gushing slit so erratically, that her pants had shimmied down around her hips in retreat. "Yes, yes, yes," she chanted, urging him on as the pads of his fingers rotated her swollen clitoris round and round, up and down, and side to side. She was panting like a dog, this close to exploding from the inside out and flooding his palm with her honey. The little angel perched on one of her shoulders was outraged. *Elise, you should be ashamed of yourself! Look at you!* But the little devil perched on her other shoulder couldn't have cared less. *Well, it's about time*, it purred gleefully. *Loosen up for once in your life and just...enjoy. We deserve this!*

"Elise, are you listening?"

"Yes...y-yes. I'm l-listening."

"Liar," he said, dropping to his knees behind her. He dragged her jeans down to her ankles as he went and then promptly pushed his face into the valley between her naked butt cheeks. Inhaling deeply, he palmed her flesh, separated it and then plunged his long, stiff tongue into her pulsing sheath from behind over and over again until her knees buckled. When she began sinking to the ground this time, he let her go, guiding her into the kind of free fall that flattened her palms on the wet grass in front of her and bent her knees at just the right angle to allow him full access from behind.

Elise's eyes rolled up into her head and a primal

scream shot out of her mouth. The exquisite clamp of Broderick's lips and tongue around her twitching clitoris was nearly too intense to withstand, especially when he tugged on it gently once, twice, and then three times, and sent her blasting off into orbit.

Elise was asleep.

Dead to the world asleep.

Which was good for her because Broderick was wide-awake, his cock was bobbing in the air like a Louisville Slugger and the woman currently snuggled up with at least two pillows and a mountain of twisted, tangled covers on the king-size bed was completely and utterly irresistible to him. She was much safer asleep.

He caught himself prowling around the perimeter of the bed for the tenth time, hoping that she'd wake up soon so he could ride her right back to dreamland, and told himself to chill out. After the night they'd had, she was exhausted. Letting her sleep in peace was the right thing to do, particularly since he was mostly to blame for her present comatose-like state. Not that he felt even a little bit guilty about it, but there it was—a sliver of the single ounce of humanity that he'd managed to hang on to despite it all. A willing sacrifice just for her, because they hadn't stopped off at just one place on the way home, but more like three, counting the suite at the Hilton, and he still had yet to deliver her to her doorstep.

Naked except for the Audemars Piguet watch on his wrist, which he'd put on out of habit after rolling out of bed a while ago, Broderick decided to retreat from the bedroom and the sleeping temptress within it. He grabbed his jeans from the floor by the bed on his way out of the room and pulled the door closed behind him. In search of food, he hopped into his jeans on his way across the sitting room to raid the leftovers on their room-service lunch cart. Finding only fruit, he placed the cover back on the serving dish, settled for a beer from the minibar and picked up the television remote. He dropped into a chair across from the flat-screen television and switched it on, frowning when Dr. Phil's face filled the screen.

Was it any wonder that his thoughts immediately started wandering?

You are the most beautiful woman I've ever seen.

Hearing his own breathless, shuddering voice say those words aloud as he was slowly bouncing Elise up and down on his throbbing cock had been every bit as exciting for him as hearing them clearly was for her. He had no sooner finished whispering them in her ear, when her pulsing walls suddenly clenched his shaft in a velvet choke hold and her throaty moans had grown louder. With her eyes narrowed to slits in her flushed face, her head lolling sideways on her neck and her mouth hanging open in a perpetual O of surprised pleasure, she looked like an addict in the throes of a rhapsodic high. *Shh*, he had whispered into her mouth between long, deep strokes. *You'll wake up the owner of this barn and get us both arrested. Or killed*, he remembered thinking as his eyes slid closed, his tongue uncurled against hers and every muscle in his body stiffened.

Her bra and sweater were hanging from one of her wrists because that was as far as they'd gotten before patience with them had run out, and her pants and underwear were dangling from one of her ankles because that was as far as they'd gotten before patience with her second shoe had run out. They were in a random stranger's dark, deserted barn, one they'd passed en route back to the interstate, and his own pants were pooled around his ankles. He was buried so deeply inside her tight sheath that she was anchored to the wall and the sounds coming out of her mouth were getting louder and louder by the second. Theirs was definitely not a good look for a suspicious and potentially trigger-happy farmer to stumble upon in the middle of the night.

Broderick blinked out of his pornographic thoughts just in time to see that Dr. Phil's guest was the one and only Dr. Ruth. He swallowed a mouthful of beer and grinned, wondering what the renowned sex therapist would think about two responsible adults ducking into the back row of an all-night movie theater and necking throughout the entire foreign feature, subtitles and all. Her with as much of his penis as possible wrapped in her fist and him with both of her cloud-soft breasts in his mouth damn near at the same time. The theater was sparsely populated, with only a handful of other viewers filling a small cluster of seats down front, and, after discovering that Elise had never made out in a movie theater, it couldn't have worked out better for them if he'd planned it.

He chuckled into his beer and then tilted the bottle again, drinking long and deep.

It was almost dawn when they had finally stumbled into the Hilton's lobby, and well after seven in the morning when they fell into bed, still wet from a shared shower and too sleepy to care about food. And even then, at least another hour had passed before they had actually gotten around to sleeping.

So, yeah, Elise deserved some uninterrupted rest. He couldn't remember the last time he'd had any himself, but she wasn't him. She led a charmed, organized life, both personally and professionally. He, on the other hand, had been known to go days without food or sleep when he was on assignment, depending on where he was, whom he was keeping company with and whether or not it was safe to partake in either. Regardless of what the pretty Miss Carrington made her luscious mouth say, her brand of private investigations was galaxies away from his. She was normal and she needed rest. He was not and could not recall the last time, before today, that he'd enjoyed such a luxury.

He glanced at his watch. Dusk had come and gone, though, and, except to eat lunch, Elise had slept the day away. If his own stomach was rumbling nonstop, which it was, then hers had to be, too. Room service was always an option, but he was aroused again and suddenly restless. He needed something, anything, to do with himself that didn't involve prowling around a hotel room, lusting after a sexual neophyte who had somehow given him the best fling sex that he'd ever had.

As if in solidarity with his thoughts, his cock twitched. Determined to ignore it, he set his beer on a side table and glanced at his watch. To hell with it. He'd give Elise fifteen more minutes, and then he was going to wake her up by any means necessary.

The sound of his ringing cell phone rolled him to his feet and sent him hurrying quietly into the bedroom to answer it before it woke Elise. Relieved to see that she hadn't stirred, he snatched it from the nightstand, silenced it and took it back into the sitting room with him.

"Cannon," he barked into the phone as soon as the bedroom door was closed behind him.

"Cannon, it's Leahy. Hold up a sec, while I scramble the line." The line went silent for several seconds, and then Leahy was back. "Well, well, well." His deep voice drifted through the phone. "Looks like the dead has finally risen."

"Funny," Broderick drawled, grinning as he resumed his seat and stretched his legs out in front of him. "Not that I owe you any explanations, but I'm sure I told you I'd be off the grid for the next couple of days. What's up, Leahy? You miss me already?" Patrick Leahy was the very first field agent that Broderick had recruited when he first started Cannon Corp. After being wounded during his fourth tour in Afghanistan and then honorably discharged from the army, Patrick had come through physical therapy with flying colors and been anxious to get back to work. Not only were his credentials rock solid and his references impeccable, but he was an expert marksman and a ride-or-die soldier. Broderick had gambled on him and somewhere along the way, he'd become as indispensable as Broderick's right hand. That didn't mean he wasn't an occasional pain in the ass, though.

"Hell, no," Leahy shot back. "Do you know how many parties we've thrown since you've been gone? Dude, please. I just thought I'd make sure you were still breathing, that's all. Plus, somebody had to call and tell you that it looks like you're going to have to cut your couple of days off the grid short. Delgado's already called twice today, requesting that you get in contact with him as soon as possible. Seems he's ready to talk extraction and he needs you to make it happen for him."

"I could've sworn that I assigned Morganford and Delaney to Delgado's situation." Delgado, an Argentinian Federal Court Judge, had recently been appointed to the bench and his political career looked promising. Then he'd had the misfortune of presiding over the trial of a high-ranking member of a notoriously violent drug cartel out of Buenos Aires. Unfortunately for him, the judge's views about mandatory sentencing for drug offenders were some of the harshest around. But the abduction of his wife and eleven-year-old son this morning, shortly after the defendant learned of his guilty verdict, was forcing him to reconsider his views before he and the other two presiding judges handed down a sentence. If he wanted his family back, the defendant's freedom was the trade-off.

The sentencing hearing was scheduled for less than two weeks away, and, naturally, Delgado wanted his family safe and out of the country long before it all went down. Once it did, Broderick would close his case altogether by facilitating Delgado's secret relocation, as well. For Delgado, trusting his own government to keep him safe wasn't even an option, especially since the other two judges involved were shaking in their boots, too.

"You did, and that's exactly what I told him. However, he doesn't want Morganford and Delaney. He wants you to lead the team going in and coming out."

"How soon is he ready to move?"

"Yesterday, so what should I tell him?"

Movement in Broderick's peripheral vision caught his attention, and he turned to watch a sleepy-eyed, rosy-cheeked Elise emerge from the bedroom wrapped in a bedsheet. Noticing that he was on a call, she stopped short, pointed to her tummy and then rubbed it in a universal "I'm hungry" sign. He smiled at the picture she made, with her hair flying wildly around her face in a frizzy golden halo, the sheet dragging the floor behind her and an utterly feline gleam in her eyes. She looked like the proverbial cat who'd eaten the canary.

He shifted the phone away from his mouth. "What are you in the mood for?" he asked Elise.

"What?" Leahy asked in his ear.

"Not you," he growled.

"I don't know, maybe something light, since we had pasta for lunch?"

"Tell you what, you have something light, while I have a steak. I thought maybe we'd go out to dinner. Is that okay with you?"

"So that's why you've been missing in action," Leahy said as if he'd finally just solved an elusive mystery. "You suddenly got a woman stashed away somewhere, Cannon?"

"Uh, no, and shut up."

Leahy chuckled.

"What?" Elise asked, looking confused.

"Not you, gorgeous."

"Gorgeous?" Leahy sounded suspicious. "You have a pet name for her, too? Interesting."

"Oh." Elise looked even more confused. "Why don't I just wait for you in there?" Elise asked, pointing to the bedroom doorway behind her.

"I'll be right there," he called after her. As soon as the bedroom door closed, he turned his attention back to his cell. "Contact Delgado and set up a follow-up meeting with him for tomorrow evening. We'll take the jet and go to him."

"Wait a second, *we?*"

"Hell, yeah. You didn't seriously think that I was about to infiltrate Argentinian drug cartel territory with my ass hanging out, did you? If I go in, I'm taking you and Rodriguez with me."

"Did you forget that Rodriguez is out on maternity leave until the week after next?"

"Shit." Amelia Rodriguez was a master at kicking asses first and taking names later, exactly the kind of agent that you wanted watching your back when it counted. "I did forget, though I don't know how since I was at her daughter's christening."

"And you're the baby's honorary uncle. Damn, if I ever have kids, remind me not to ask you to do anything except change crappy diapers."

"Whatever. Pull Johannes off of the Libertine assignment and bring him in. I'll be back at headquarters by tomorrow afternoon at the latest. We'll take the jet from there."

"Got it."

"Later," Broderick said and ended the call. It was time to get back work. That was a good thing, right?

Chapter 11

The pickings for gourmet dining in Columbia, Missouri, were slim, but Elise and Broderick lucked out when they strolled into a dark, sophisticated little cave of a place called Sophia's. Against the backdrop of edgy music, exposed brick walls and dim lighting, white-shirted servers navigated the sea of tables in the main dining area seamlessly. For a Wednesday night, the crowd was sizable and lively, but they were still fortunate enough to snag a corner booth near the bar without having to wait very long. Which was great, because Elise was starving. Her original plan to have something light for dinner went right out the window as soon as she inhaled the mouth-watering aromas wafting in the air and spied the array of artfully arranged entrées on a passing server's loaded-down tray.

"I think I know what I want," she said, setting aside the leather-bound menu that she'd been perusing carefully for the past several minutes and meeting Broderick's eyes.

"It wouldn't be the pan-seared ahi tuna, would it?"

Elise's face dissolved into a pleased smile. "How did you know?"

"Lucky guess," Broderick said, staring at her as he picked up his water glass and sipped. "Plus, your lips move when you read silently. Did you know that?"

God, he was a beautiful man. Did *he* know that? "No, I didn't." She felt her face heat up and cursed herself. "I always tease Olivia for doing the same thing. No wonder she just laughs and flips me the bird every time."

"She's a character," Broderick commented, flashing her a smile that immediately tightened her nipples.

She smothered a sigh of relief when their server appeared at the edge of their table, granting her a temporary reprieve from having an audience when she blushed, yet again, like a sixteen-year-old. She sipped from her water glass while he ordered pan-seared ahi Tuna and a glass of Riesling for her, and a brandy-cream filet mignon and a glass of Cabernet Sauvignon for himself, and hoped that her face returned to normal before their server moved away.

"So, what was it like growing up with a twin?" he asked when they were alone again.

Elise set her glass down slowly, thinking carefully about the question and how best to answer it. "For me," she began thoughtfully, "I guess it was a little bit like growing up alongside my own personal idol. While I was studying, Olivia was watching the clock, waiting for our parents to fall asleep, so she could borrow one of their cars and sneak out to an all-night party somewhere. I followed the rules and she made up her own as she went along. And there wasn't a punishment on the table that she couldn't negotiate favorable terms for herself within or talk herself out of completely, depending on how many hours of sleep she'd had the night before."

Broderick laughed. "She sounds like a real badass."

"She was," Elise agreed, laughing, too. "I sort of lived vicariously through her, you know? She did all the stuff that I was too afraid to do, and then she shared every last detail about it with me, so it was like I was there, doing it, too. Except I didn't have to suffer the consequences of her actions."

"But you suffered anyway, didn't you?"

"Of course," she conceded with a giggle. "I felt sorry for her, so I kept her company during her many, many, *many* groundings. That's how she met Joel, actually. My parents were out of town for New Year's, and she snuck out to a New Year's Eve party at a club downtown. Joel was there and the rest, as they say, is history."

"Wait a minute, Joel and Olivia were an item?" He was incredulous, staring at Elise with wide eyes and his mouth hanging open.

"Oh my God, yes! They were madly in love and almost got married. Joel didn't tell you?"

"I was the one who introduced him to *Heather* in the first place, so I don't remember the topic ever coming up."

Elise pretended to scratch her head in amused confusion. "Hmm, guess not, huh?" she said and they both cracked up. "If you ever tell her I said this, I'll deny it with everything in me, but I've always envied her complete and utter disregard for other people's opinions, mine included. Take Joel, for instance. When they first started dating, I hounded her for days about him being too old, too advanced for her, too…everything. What if you get pregnant, I said? What if his parents don't like you because you're black, I said? She listened for a while and then she said 'Elise, you're my sister and I love you. But this is my life. That's all the explanation you or anyone else needs.' After that, I couldn't figure out whether I wanted to strangle her or *be* her."

"So she carried the pitchfork and you wore the halo. Did you switch places for tests and final exams, the way twins always do in the movies, too?"

"Oh, no. I was way too serious about my academic career to risk getting caught doing something like that," Elise said, sitting back to make room on the tabletop for her wineglass when she spied their oncoming server. "Thank you," she said as a linen coaster and then a tall glass of chilled white wine was placed in front of her.

"Your entrées should be out shortly. Can I get either of you anything else in the meantime?"

Elise shook her head at Broderick's silent query. "I think we're fine for now, thank you," he told the woman as she set his wineglass in front of him. As soon as she was gone again, he turned back to Elise with his brows cocked. "You were saying?"

"Just that I was a militant nerd and Olivia wasn't. She fooled around so much throughout high school that

I don't even want to think about how she managed to get passing grades the whole time. My parents were sure that she'd eventually end up in prison for running some sort of black-book escort agency, and, I have to admit, I wouldn't have been all that surprised myself if she had. She's always been for making love, not war, so, I figured, she'd get herself into some kind of world-wide sex scandal and I, being fresh out of law school and ready to take on the world by then, would have to save her ass. I guess you can see that things didn't quite work out that way. Her SAT scores were actually better than mine."

"Did she go to Northwestern, too?"

Elise shook her head as she swallowed a mouthful of wine. "Loyola. She studied chemistry. Turns out, she was a closet nerd all along. Who knew that it was possible to be serious about education and be a party girl at the same time?"

His eyebrows shot up again and a smile toyed with his lips. "It's not?"

"I never thought so before."

"What do you think now?"

"Now, I'm wondering why I never thought about starting my own black-book escort agency. I could've easily overseen the day-to-day operations between classes or after work."

Broderick had been in the midst of taking a sip of wine when Elise shared her latest revelation and clearly it caught him off guard. He quickly set his glass down and snatched up a linen napkin from the table, pressing it to his mouth while he worked out swallowing without choking himself and breathing at the same time. Several seconds passed with him struggling to clear his throat.

"Why is that so shocking?" She wasn't sure if she was amused or offended.

"It's not." He cleared his throat one last time and reached for his water glass. "In fact, it's actually kind of arousing," he murmured as he put the glass to his mouth and sipped. "But then, so is the fact that, at this very moment, I happen to be the only man on Earth who knows that your clitoris is pierced with a tiny pink diamond. So I might be a little biased, either way."

"I was wondering how long it would take you to get around to mentioning that."

He cracked a smile. "You knew I would."

Her genital piercing was only six months old and, until Broderick, only she and her vibrator knew it existed. "No one else knows about it, not even Olivia, so if I ever hear about it somewhere else, I'll know it came from you."

"And no one ever will," he put in quickly, staving off the rest of her tirade with his hands up in mock supplication. "Your secret is safe with me. I only brought it up to point out something that's very obvious to me."

"Which is?"

"Which is that it's okay to keep some things secret and sacred. Personally, I'm glad you were a nerd growing up."

"Why?"

"Because it means you gave me something that very few people have ever been given. From where I'm sitting, that's considered a gift. As a matter of fact, everything about these past couple of days with you has been incredible. So here's another secret for you, Elise. Your diamond-studded clit is the sweetest that I've ever had the distinct pleasure of tasting, and, despite what you might be thinking, there haven't been very many. If I ever hear that somewhere else," he said, gesturing across the table at her with his wineglass before sipping. "I'll know it was you."

If their server was aware of the tension between them when she reappeared just then with their entrées, she didn't let on. If she noticed that they seemed to be hypnotized by each other's gazes, she didn't comment as she set their plates before them, politely asked if they'd like anything else and eventually drifted away when it finally occurred to Broderick to shake his head in response.

Has been. He'd said *has been.* The subtle difference in tenses hadn't escaped Elise's notice. As turned-on as she was by Broderick's admission, she couldn't help feeling an accompanying wave of disappointment. She'd known all along that what they were doing was temporary, that they'd part ways and probably never see each other again after it was over. But now that the time had apparently come, she wasn't as ready to be done with it or with him as she thought she'd be.

She could hear Olivia now. *Suck it up, Elise. This is why they're called flings, remember?*

Yes, and this is also why I've avoided them like the plague, she mentally countered.

She was the first to look away, picking up the linen

napkin beside her plate and transferring it to her lap. "When do we leave?"

"First thing in the morning" came his quiet reply.

"Then I guess we should hurry and finish up here, so we can get back to the hotel and get some sleep. You probably want to get an early start." She picked up her knife and fork and cut into her tuna steak.

"Not too early, I hope."

Her eyes flickered up to his and instantly went liquid with arousal when she saw the raw desire on his face. "No...not too early. Oh, and, by the way," she whispered as she forked up a morsel of tuna and offered it to him across the table. His full lips closed around her fork just as she said, "Did I mention that I'm not wearing any panties?"

A redhead walked out of the ladies' room first and then, finally, the brunette that Broderick had been watching for, for the past sixty seconds. Once she was out of sight, he stepped from the shadows and slipped through the door before it closed after her. Locking it behind him, he met Elise's saucer-sized eyes in the mirror in front of her at the vanity and put his index finger to his lips. "Shh," he warned her horror-stricken reflection, then disappeared down the walkway fronting a row of stalls. Finding them all empty, he returned, walking up behind Elise at the mirror and parking his lips next to her ear. The lip-gloss wand in her hand froze halfway to her mouth.

"Was there any particular reason you felt it necessary to mention to me that you weren't wearing panties?" he growled against the shell of her ear. Needing to see for himself, he reached down and slowly lifted the hem of her skirt until it was gathered around her waist and he could see her smooth-shaven mound clearly in the mirror in front of them.

Reaching around her, he slowly sank his middle finger into her slit and dragged the pad of his finger back and forth across her swollen clitoris.

She gasped. "Oh, God, Broderick. You can't do this to me here. Someone might be waiting to come in." He hit a sweet spot and her hips bucked, mouth fell open. "Oooh, that feels so good." She covered his hand with hers and slowly rocked her hips in sync with the rhythm of his finger's strokes.

His penis bone hard and pulsing wildly inside his Brooks Brother's trousers, Broderick watched Elise's face closely in the mirror, enjoying the play of sensations that randomly darted across her face. Fear that they would be caught warred with the excitement of struggling to keep her eyes open so she could watch his fingers play between her slick lips. She was wet and the fact that she could see for herself just how wet she was every time his finger plunged deep and then withdrew, coated with her glistening juices, seemed to ramp up her excitement that much more. As a result, his own excitement shot through the roof.

"You're so goddamn beautiful when you cum. Did you know that? You're not wearing panties because you want me to suck your clit until you cum, isn't that right, Elise?"

"Oh, God, yes," she pleaded, catching his eyes in the mirror. "Yes!"

"All right, but only if you promise not to scream."

"I won't," she promised breathlessly.

"Turn around then." She did and he quickly lifted her and set her butt on the edge of the vanity top. She instinctively leaned back against the mirror as he parted her thighs. "That's a good girl," he crooned as he dropped down to his haunches between them and inhaled the aroma of her dripping sex deep into his nostrils. "Have I told you yet exactly how much seeing your bare pussy turns me on?"

"N-no," Elise whispered.

"No?" He dipped his head and dragged the flat of his tongue across her honey-soaked slit, chuckling when her thighs began trembling. "Then allow me show you," he said, spreading her lips open and homing in on the pink pearl that lay within with the tip of his flickering tongue.

In two minutes flat, Broderick dropped a soft kiss on the back of Elise's neck, met her sleepy-looking, feline eyes in the mirror and whispered, "Meet you back at the table," into her ear. Then he unlocked the bathroom door and slipped out as quickly as he'd slipped in.

He was in trouble, that much was obvious, even to someone as pussy whipped as he admittedly was. The problem, if you could call it that, was that he couldn't quite figure out how to snap himself out of the spell that Elise Carrington had somehow cast on him. Or if he even wanted to.

Nah, that wasn't really the problem. Time, distance

and throwing himself into his work would take care of his insatiable sex drive easily enough. They always did. The real problem was that she was so damn irresistible in the here and now. He liked to give her a hard time about her constant blushing because it only made her blush more. But in reality, if blushes equaled hardons, then he was no better than she was at concealing his body's reaction to her. One look, one slant of those incredibly expressive tigress eyes in his direction, and he was ready to do whatever he had to do for a taste of her lips or a lick of her silky skin—for the privilege of burying himself balls deep in her heat and riding her until he was slick with sweat and ready to pass out.

Broderick adored women and he loved sex. He'd had plenty of it over the years, and, God willing, he'd have plenty more before it was all over. But this…whatever this was that he and Elise Carrington were doing was starting to wander over into more-than-sex territory, and that was the real problem. He wasn't supposed to want her this much, and being with her definitely wasn't supposed to feel so good.

Yep, he was definitely in trouble. Not a lot of trouble, all things considered, but enough that he considered Leahy's summons a lucky break. The sooner he got the hell out of Dodge, the better. Admitting that he had a problem was the first step. A few days spent lurking in the shadows of an Argentinian ghetto would surely take care of the rest.

Chapter 12

Olivia's face was the first thing Elise saw when she walked through the door at home.

"Well, well, well, if it isn't our very own Lady Chatterley," Olivia drawled sarcastically, strolling across the foyer in Elise's direction with her arms folded underneath her breasts and her reading glasses perched on the tip of her nose. She stared at Elise over the hot-pink rim. "You look very...satisfied. Did you enjoy yourself?"

"Uh..." Suddenly wary, Elise watched Olivia's face carefully as she hung her jacket in the coat closet, searching for clues as to how she should respond. By itself, the question seemed innocent enough, but Olivia's tone was off and so was her demeanor. "I guess so, yes."

"Good," Olivia chirped. "I'm glad you enjoyed yourself. That's what it looked like when I peeked out the window just now and saw you two together. I thought, wow, it's about time Elise got her groove back. Then I thought, well, it's not like she ever really had a groove in the first place, but that doesn't matter right now. What matters is that she finally got some. I just hope it was enough to last you for a while because, after today, you can never see or talk to Broderick Cannon again. Whatever just happened between the two of you, as of right this second, is over. It has to be."

Elise was stunned, looking at Olivia like she'd lost her mind. "What are you talking about?"

"What am I talking about?" Olivia unfolded an arm to scratch her head as if it would help her think faster. "Well, let's see…" She started pacing back and forth nervously in front of Elise, who noticed the manila folder tucked underneath her folded arm on Olivia's third pass. "You know how we sometimes make women in desperate situations disappear from one place and then help them reappear someplace else as a completely different person?"

Oh, God, no.

"Yes," Elise heard herself say.

It can't be.

But Elise somehow knew that it was long before Olivia spoke and confirmed her worst fears. After all, wasn't this exactly the kind of luck that she always seemed to attract?

"We erased eight women back in 2013. Guess who was one of them?" Olivia announced as she handed over the folder she was holding, pushed her glasses higher up on the bridge of her nose and then refolded her arms smartly. "Brandy Cannon was, Elise. You bet the man that you could find the sister he's been searching for, for three years and, as it turns out, you and I are the reason she went missing to begin with."

Karma was a bitch.

Elise had always known that. But, still. There was nothing like a head-on collision with the lady herself to really drive the point home. One minute, she was floating on cloud nine, enjoying the kind of sex-induced high that she'd only heard about from other women, and the next, she was trying to make a deal with the devil for a do-over, a chance to refuse Joel's case—*again*—and stick to her guns this time.

"I knew I shouldn't have taken Joel's case," she said, pushing aside one of several shoe boxes lined up on a shelf in her bedroom closet and pressing her index finger to the small pane of glass that the shift revealed. After a series of short beeps, during which time an electronic device on the other side of the wall scanned her fingerprint to confirm her identity, the false wall to her left unlocked in silent welcome. She pushed gently and the panel swung open, taking two rows of neatly hung blouses with it and revealing the hidden room behind it. "Thank you, again, for that, by the way," she said, stepping through the doorway and activating the motion-sensitive overhead lighting.

Olivia barged through the doorway right behind her, tossing the manila folder in her hand on the glass-topped conference table in the center of the room, then slapping her hands on her hips and rounding on Elise. "I've already apologized six times now, sis. Doing it once more isn't going to make me feel any worse, but it will piss me off. This is no more my fault than it is yours. It could've happened to either of us and you know it." Sidestepping Elise, she rounded the table and switched on the flat-screen monitor on the far wall. "Frankly," she said as she scanned the color-coded tabbed options already on display there, "I'm surprised it hasn't already."

Elise pulled a leather chair away from the table and dropped into it heavily, sliding the folder across the table in her direction and flipping it open on the table-top in front of her. "Start from the beginning, please, so I can wrap my head around this nightmare."

As deeply offended as she'd pretended to be when Broderick had confronted her, he'd really only been slightly incorrect in suggesting that she spent most of her investigative time tracking down errant husbands. It wasn't something that she liked to dwell on, but she did, in fact, log a decent number of billable hours following philandering spouses around and gathering ammunition for nasty divorces. Certainly not *all* of her billable hours, but enough of them to satisfy their tax accountant, the IRS and any other legal entity that cared to look closely at their daily operations. Those hours, as well as the ones they logged while working missing persons cases, were the very things that lent Carrington Consulting both the credibility and the invisibility that it required in order to continue flying under the radar— undetected and undisturbed.

The real work, though, was done right here in their secret war room, away from the eyes and ears of the rest of the world. It wasn't included on any blueprint of the house in existence, and, other than the two of them, no one else knew that it was there, which was a good thing because, if it was ever discovered, theirs and several other heads across the country would roll. The last time Elise had bothered to check, helping battered women walk away from their current lives and making them disappear into thin air was a crime. And orange, she thought with a shudder of revulsion, had never been her color.

"As you wish," Olivia said, detaching a remote from the side panel of the monitor, aiming it at the screen and then stepping aside as several different images expanded to fill the seventy-two-inch space in a checkerboard pattern. "This is Brandy Melissa Cannon Dortch," she said, enlarging the first image—a professional portrait of the woman in question. It was the same photo as the one that Broderick had shown her, but, for some reason, Elise was just now clearly seeing the shared resemblance.

"At the time of her disappearance three years ago, she was the forty-four-year-old wife of Dennis Dortch." She glanced back at Elise over her shoulder and smirked. "He was the forty-eight-year-old mayor of Los Angeles, California, then and just beginning his second term." A second image came forward, setting up a side-by-side photo comparison. "As you can see, they were a stylish interracial couple, so their marriage was sort of like a political poster child for racial tolerance, which, since Barack Obama was on the scene, as well, was sort of the country's collective theme song at the time. It's also a

large part of the reason why a fairly unknown city councilman, which Dortch was up until early 2007, when
he suddenly appeared on the local political scene and
announced his intended candidacy in the city's 2008
mayoral election, gained a majority of the minority vote
and won the election by a very skinny margin. Not long
after, Brandy gave up her position with LA's branch
of the Federal Reserve. He was reelected for a second
term in 2012, and then Brandy came to us through the
network in 2013. She and Dortch had been married for
ten years by then."

Elise studied Brandy's photo then looked down at the
contents of the folder. Flipping through a sheaf of paper-
clipped documents, she paid special attention to the photo-
copied medical records and color photos from a variety of
doctor and hospital visits. Over a ten-year period, Brandy
had received medical treatment for an array of physical
injuries, ranging from very minor to extremely serious.
The first time was for a broken pinkie toe six months
after her wedding, and the last time for a broken jaw just
months before she disappeared. In between those visits,
she'd been seen several times by plastic surgeons, for re-
constructive surgeries to her face, and twice by an oral
surgeon for dental implants. Like many of the women
they serviced, these visits had always occurred in private
office settings or on an outpatient basis, but never in a
traditional hospital setting, where her constant and esca-
lating injuries were likely to draw unwanted attention.

"Dortch was smart," Olivia said, breaking into
Elise's thoughts. "And they were fairly comfortable financially, so arranging private doctor visits for his wife

or a discreet procedure here and there was likely just a matter of making a few phone calls or snapping his fingers at the right people."

Elise looked up from the file and frowned at Dortch's image on the screen. He was handsome, if you liked beady green eyes and tight mouths, she thought and nearly snarled. The man had beaten his wife mercilessly for a decade and had somehow convinced her to put on a brave, happy face for the world through it all. He was a wolf in sheep's clothing.

"You keep saying 'was.' What happened to him?" she asked.

"He was killed by a hit-and-run driver less than a week before Brandy came to us," Olivia supplied, aiming the remote at the screen. A second tab expanded over the first one. "News of the accident was covered by several of the major media outlets. Here's a clip from one of the local nightly news broadcasts." She pressed another button, and an embedded video began playing in the top right corner of the screen. After it ended, she expanded another tab on the screen. "His death was ruled an accident and the investigation was quickly and quietly closed. Given that he was dead and she was finally free of his abuse, Brandy had no reason to contact us, except she knew that her husband's death wasn't an accident and that she was next. That brings us around to the *why* of it all." She pressed a button and a new image took over the screen.

Seeing it, Elise groaned and dropped her head in her hands. A second later, her head popped back up. "Are you kidding me?" she shrieked incredulously at Olivia.

"Please tell me that's not Borya Maysak." Maysak was a notorious Russian mob figure. It was impossible for anyone who followed the international news channels on at least a part-time basis not to recognize him on sight.

"It is." Olivia's voice held a note of finality. "For years, there were rumors that Dortch was mixed up with the Russian mafia and I have to admit it does make sense, when I think about how quickly he ended up in elected office. As I said, before running, Dortch was a city councilman, but he put food on the family table as a financial advisor for one of those chain operations. The rumors were never confirmed, but, according to Eli's intel, Maysak was behind Dortch's campaign funding, among other things, during his term and, in exchange, Dortch was behind the disappearance of five million dollars of Maysak's dirty money. The poor idiot was supposed to be laundering it, but he got sticky fingers, instead. In the broad scheme of things, five million is pocket change to Maysak but, for someone like him, it's the principle of the matter. He would've wanted to send a message."

"Dortch's death was a hit," Elise said, more to herself than to Olivia. "I remember bits and pieces of the story now. It broke around the same time that the California wildfires were dominating the news. I remember thinking at the time that it didn't get nearly as much coverage as it should have."

"You're right, it didn't. Lucky for us, that worked in our favor. By all indications, Brandy was next on Maysak's hit list. There was some speculation that she knew about the theft and possibly had a hand in it. Plus, she

had intimate knowledge of her husband's business dealings with Maysak. The morning that she came to us,
her house had been broken into by two men that she'd
never seen before, while she was out running errands.
She watched the whole thing on her cell phone, via the
closed-circuit cameras that Dortch had the foresight to
install when they bought the place. She never returned
home. Instead she hid out in a local women's shelter
for a couple of days and then someone slipped her a
network green card. That's how she found us. While
all of the major networks were covering her disappearance and speculating on what happened to her, she was
moving through the network. When no credible leads
ever turned up, her digital footprint eventually disappeared and, when no body was ever found, the case
went cold." The heels of her stiletto pumps clicked on
the tile floor as she slowly paced from one end of the
screen to the other. "Facial recognition software posi-
tively identified the two men as two of Maysak's goons,
so she knew what was up."

"If we erased her to save her life, then I should remember her more clearly. It's interesting that I don't."
Closing the folder, Elise sat back in her chair and
threaded her fingers through her hair.

How could this be happening?

"You had just taken on a child abduction case in
Florida, so you were only around for the initial news
coverage. If you met her in person, it would've only
been once or twice and, even then, only in passing,"
Olivia explained, leaning a hip against the table. Turning back to the screen, she studied the images there in

silence for several seconds. "I processed her and handled her placement myself. By the time you were done with your case in Florida, Brandy Cannon Dortch had already ceased to exist. I wonder if she used Maysak's dirty money to cover our fee."

Elise sent her sister a withering look. "That's the last thing we should be worried about right now. I'm more interested in knowing how much Broderick knows."

"Maysak is a dangerous man and he's powerful, but men like him don't get that way by being fools. I did some more digging on your man while you were gone. Believe me, Maysak wouldn't have wanted the kind of attention that messing with him would've resulted in."

"He's not my man."

Olivia flapped a dismissive hand. "Whatever. Maysak would've been meticulous enough in his own research to find out for himself that Broderick was out of the country, as well as out of contact with his sister both before and after the money went missing. They were born ten years apart, and, by Brandy's own admission, they weren't very close. She probably didn't think Broderick would even miss her enough to bother looking for her."

"Great," Elise chirped with sarcastic cheer. "That eliminates Broderick as a potential target, but what about us?" Visions of bloody shoot-outs, duct-taped mouths and dark vans flashed before her eyes. "Maysak is probably sitting back somewhere, following Broderick's progress and waiting for the trail he leaves to lead him right to Brandy. That's what I would do, if I were him. And if it ever does lead to her and she talks—"

"It won't," Olivia cut in sharply. "And, hell, even if it does, except for what's in that folder and the few details that I can recall from memory, there's nothing concrete linking us to Brandy Cannon Dortch's disappearance."

In the interest of plausible deniability, the data that they retained on erasures was purposely vague. Aside from the numerically coded files that they maintained on each client's abuse history, there was nothing else in their physical possession that could or would reveal anything else about the women they helped. Everything was kept in this room and stored only on the devices within it, and all of it within arm's reach of quick and permanent disposal at a moment's notice. Elise was well aware of the safeguard procedures they had put into place when they first started out. But Borya Maysak wasn't someone that she wanted to come face-to-face with, now or ever.

"Where is Brandy now?"

"Well, as you know, she started out in Albuquerque, New Mexico, but she requested relocation about a year ago, after a new tenant moved into her building and spooked her. Per Brandy's report, the new tenant started asking too many questions and poking around in her things when she thought Brandy wasn't paying attention. I don't yet know where she ended up after that. But I put Eli on her trail as soon as I found out who and what she was, and he's working his way through the network now. We should have an exact location on her in a couple of hours."

"Why so long?"

"Delays are a part of the process, remember?"

Elise sighed disgustedly. "How could I forget? I helped design the process."

The network was still in its infancy when she'd first stumbled upon it. Well, technically, *she* hadn't stumbled upon the network, it had actually stumbled upon *her*. By then, she'd been volunteering at the shelter for nearly a decade, having racked up thousands of frequent-flyer miles in college by coming home every chance she got, and, later, sacrificing one of every two days that she was off duty from the department to the cause. What had started as a means of completing a community service requirement for high-school graduation, had quickly become her passion. As if it was precisely what she'd been born to do and fate had simply brought her to it when it was time to begin doing it. Which, as fate would have it, was right around the time that the police commissioner's wife was tried and convicted of murdering the abusive monster that was her husband.

Working at the shelter, Elise had heard so many stories of torture and unspeakable violence that for months, she'd had nightmares. Some of the women found the strength to get out, and, with support from friends and family, were able to build new lives for themselves. But there were other women who wanted to get out and couldn't, because they had nowhere to turn for help. Women who eventually gave up on the possibility of escape and faded into the shadows, where they silently screamed in terror each and every day.

The very first woman that she and Olivia had erased was the wife of a four-star general, and for twenty years, she had suffered her abuser's torture in silence. Until the day the general lodged a steak knife in her chest, missing a major artery by a hair, because his steak was well-done, instead of medium-well, the way he preferred it. She'd tried to leave him four different times before that and had been betrayed by her own family each time. The general's family was old money, and he'd always been very generous with his in-laws, so their allegiance was to him. He made sure that she had no friends and didn't socialize outside the home, and after a while, she stopped fighting it and him. For all of that, her consolation prize was a steak knife through her chest and a near-death experience. It wasn't until a social worker slipped into her hospital room the night before she was to be discharged and sent back to her life, to offer her a second chance, that she finally got the help she needed.

Those were the kinds of women that Elise had signed on to help when she'd been approached by a recruiter with the Federal Air Marshal Program. Someone like Brandy Cannon Dortch should never have been on their client list.

Getting to her feet, Elise closed the file and scooped it up. Tucking it underneath her arm, she glanced at Olivia on her way to the door. "Okay, fine. We wait, but please let me know the second you hear something from Eli. In the meantime, I'm tired and I could really use a shower and a glass of wine."

"You're not thinking of going to see her, are you?"

Hand on the doorknob, Elise looked back at Olivia over her shoulder. "Honestly, I don't really know what I'm thinking right now, Olivia. When I walked through the door a little while ago, I was thinking of asking

you to help me come up with a believable excuse to
see Broderick again. But now that I know that even if
I did see him again, I'd have to look him in the eyes
and lie to him, there's really no point in bothering with
that now, is there?"

"Elise—"

"Now, all I can think about is how wrong you were
before, when you said that this was no one's fault and
that it could've happened to either of us. The more
I think about it, the more I realize that this couldn't
have happened to either of us, because, unlike you, I
would've taken one look at Brandy Cannon's dossier and
known that she wasn't a suitable candidate for placement. I would've refused to meet with her outright.
You were the one who made the bad call, so when you
think about it, this is really your fault. Thanks to you,
there are some very bad people out there looking for a
suspected thief that you erroneously erased, and, when
they find her, it'll only be a matter of time before she
sings and someone finds us."

Olivia was staring at her incredulously. "Is this about
Broderick?"

"No, this isn't about Broderick." *Was it?* "It's about
you carelessly putting our firm, our lives and our freedom in jeopardy."

For once in her life, Olivia was speechless. For several seconds, her mouth worked but no sound emerged.
"I didn't think—" she began when she found her voice.

"No, you didn't. Now we have a problem and I have
to figure out how to fix it. If that means I have to meet
with Brandy Cannon in person to do it, then, yes, I'm

thinking of going to see her. I really don't know yet. Maybe wine will help me think more clearly."

She walked out of the war room, leaving Olivia standing there looking like she herself was ready to go to war, and closed the door in her face. They didn't argue often and whenever they did, it was usually about something insignificant. But this latest feud, if you could even call it that, was a little different. Elise didn't know which she was more irritated by—the thought of having her fledgling affair smashed to pieces before it could even begin in earnest or the idea that Olivia could be so careless with the firm's livelihood.

Either way, wine was the answer.

Chapter 13

Eli was less than happy to see Elise's smiling face when he answered the knock at his apartment door two days later. It was barely eight o'clock in the morning and anyone who knew him knew that he wasn't a morning person, even though he was usually up and about hours before the sun rose. Despite the long-standing military slogan's implications, soldiers weren't the only people who accomplished more before 6:00 a.m. than most other people did all day. People like Eli Seamus were right there with them, lurking in the cybershadows, peeking into unsuspecting people's private lives and debating whether or not to wreak havoc with the press of a button, well before the sun rose. As a former CIA agent, the work was fun, an entertaining pastime that just happened to pay handsomely, without all the aggravation of rush-hour traffic and missed lunch breaks. As a result, he rarely ever left his apartment and never when it meant that he'd have to mingle with other people on anything other than a very small scale and for a very short period of time. The flip side was that he very rarely welcomed visitors to his home, making Elise fear that he was in danger of becoming a hermit.

A very cranky one.

"You've got ten minutes," he grumbled at Elise as he flung the door open wide enough for her to enter, whirled in his electric wheelchair and took off through the apartment.

"Well, good morning to you, too, sunshine. I brought you a gift," Elise said, stepping across the threshold and closing the door behind her.

"Oh, yeah?" he said over his shoulder. "Did you bring anything with bacon in or on it?"

"'Fraid not, my friend. Your cholesterol is through the roof and so is your blood pressure. That means no bacon for you. Just coffee." She followed him into the living room, passing him one of the two take-out coffee cups in her hands when she caught up with him and then sipping from hers carefully. It was steaming hot and strong enough to stand up and dance. He sampled his coffee, too, and promptly frowned. She'd given him her caramel latte and kept his Colombian dark roast by mistake. Wordlessly they traded cups, and she took hers over to the couch to sit.

"In that case, you only have five minutes," he said as he rolled up to a workstation in a corner of the room and pulled a keyboard from underneath the desktop. While he worked, she relaxed and enjoyed her coffee.

Eli was gruff and prickly, but his surroundings were filled with lush, lovingly tended house plants, and furniture that invited one to put up their feet and snuggle in for a nice long nap. Built-in bookshelves were crammed with books from several genres and there were framed photos of various family members, including several of his adorable granddaughter, scattered everywhere. It was such a peaceful, homey place that no one would ever suspect its sole occupant—a middle-aged, wheelchair-bound man with piercing blue eyes, a bushy gray beard and a penchant for gardening—of being a first-rate hacker and cyberspy.

"Is this a new couch?" she asked, rubbing the microsuede fabric appreciatively. "It's very nice."

"Nope," he said as his fingers flew over the keyboard. "You and Olivia still not speaking?" She'd told him about their disagreement over Brandy Cannon Dortch's erasure when she called for help.

"Nope," she parroted.

"You'll kiss and make up soon enough," Eli predicted gruffly. "In the meantime, it never hurts for any of us to be reminded to stay on our p's and q's. Speaking of which, it didn't take me long at all to get a bead on Lynn Collins," he said as he typed. The printer on the desktop next to him hummed to life and began spitting out sheets of paper. When it was done, he snatched them up and slid them into a large envelope. "Everything that you, me and God could possibly need to know about her is right here."

Elise sat up and reached for the envelope. "Any surprises that I need to know about?"

"Not really. A few blips on her credit report, a teenage arrest for shoplifting and a brother who's serving time for grand theft auto. She has a lengthy adult arrest history for petty theft and she's been under a psychiatrist's care for a personality disorder, with a secondary borderline psychosis diagnosis, since she was thirteen. Therapy, medications, the whole shebang. If you ask me, it looks like Cannon got spooked for no reason."

"That's good news, at least."

"At least," Eli agreed, spinning in his chair to face her. The expression on his face was grim. "Now on to the bad news. I agree with Olivia. There is no way in hell that you can keep seeing Cannon's brother."

Dinner, Netflix and chill. Those were Elise's plans for the rest of the evening. After meeting with Eli, she took her Jaguar in for servicing and to have the hairline scratch across the rear bumper repaired. While she waited, she borrowed a car from the dealership and crossed off a few of the other errands on her to-do list. Now that she was finally home, ordering in pizza and drowning herself in gooey cheese, extra sauce and her own private misery were next—and last—on her agenda for the day.

She hadn't heard from Broderick in two days, and that bothered her way more than it should have, considering. They barely knew each other, and they didn't owe each other anything—had never agreed to anything more than sex. But she'd been secretly hoping that he would call or text or…something. In the aftermath of their short-lived fling, her body was screaming for his touch and her vibrator was just about worn out, trying to compensate for the lack of it. It was silly to be so hung up on one man, especially at her age, but, damn, the man had given her something that no man had ever given her before—stunningly intense orgasms that somehow managed to touch every nerve ending in her body at the same glorious time.

When she looked at it like that—and she had looked at it precisely like that several times over the last forty-eight hours—the unfairness of it all was worthy of nothing less than greasy, fattening pizza, a truckload of chick flicks and, for dessert, the rest of the Rocky Road ice cream that she'd hidden in the back of the freezer.

She parked her Jaguar in the garage next to Olivia's Audi convertible and entered the house through the mudroom. In the kitchen, she set the bags in her hands on a countertop and draped her dry cleaning across the back of a chair at the kitchen table, wondering where everyone was. When she'd left this morning, both Harriet and Olivia were there. Now, even though there were still a few hours left in the workday, the house was still and quiet. She and Olivia weren't quite on speaking terms these days but if there had been a major change in plans, she would've at least sent Elise a text to let her know. Or left a—

"Note," Elise murmured to herself as her gaze landed on the handwritten note stuck to the refrigerator door with a magnet. She took it down and read Olivia's loopy text.

Sis,

A package came for you today. It looked very important and it's marked time sensitive, so, as soon as you
get home and find this, go up to your room and check
it out, please. That's where I put it—in your room.
In other news, I gave Harriet the rest of the day off
and decided to meet a friend downtown for dinner.
Be home soon.
Liv

A package? She didn't have any cases lined up that
she knew of, and she hadn't ordered anything online
or otherwise recently. *It's probably something from my
parents*, she thought as she noted the time scrawled in a
corner of the paper, then took the note with her through
the house and up the stairs to the second floor. Olivia
had left the note for her at three thirty and it was just a
few minutes past four now.

Curious to see what it could possibly be and who
could've possibly sent it, Elise walked into her bedroom
suite, saw the package awaiting her attention in the center of her bed and froze. Speechless, she stared at it as
if in a trance, her body going hot and liquid inside and
her nipples tightening. Her clit slipped out of its velvet
hood to push against the silk of her panties insistently
and her sex was suddenly engorged.

"What are you doing here?" she asked Broderick
breathlessly. *Where was her voice?*

Naked and sprawled out in the center of Elise's bed,
with one arm folded behind his head and the other extended down the length of his muscle-riddled torso,

Broderick watched Elise lazily while he massaged his erect penis rhythmically, his fingers gripping his shaft and pumping it in perfect time with his rocking hips.

"Close the door and lock it," he ordered in a strained voice. Still watching him pleasure himself, she took slow steps backward and did as she was told, returning to the foot of the bed just in time to see his mouth drop open and a bead of pre-cum appear on the tip of his sex.

They groaned simultaneously.

"What am I doing here? That's a good question," he countered huskily. "I'm supposed to be on a red-eye to Argentina right now but the funniest thing happened when I was headed to the airport." The tip of his tongue darted out to wet his lips. "Somehow, I ended up here instead. Strip for me."

Elise's hands immediately went to the buttons on her blouse and began undoing them slowly. It didn't matter why he was there. Now that he was, she intended to accept every bit of the satisfaction that he was clearly offering. She needed him inside her as soon as possible. Her blouse fell away from her shoulders, quickly followed by her bra and the few pieces of jewelry that she wore, all of it landing in a heap on the carpet at her feet. She stepped out of her pumps, and added her slacks and hair clip to the pile, staring at him the whole time. He stroked himself and stared right back.

"Two days is a long time," he said when she rolled her damp panties down her thighs and stepped out of them. "I had to see you again before I left. I'm sorry, I should've called first."

Elise climbed onto the mattress, creeping toward him on her knees. "I'm glad you came."

"Are you? Why?"

"I wanted to see you again, too." Braced on her hands and knees in the V of his thighs, she surveyed the scene before her appreciatively. He lay before her, hers for the taking, and she couldn't make up her mind about where or what to start taking first. Eventually her gaze landed on the object of her fascination—his throbbing penis—and lingered. Her mouth watered and her vision blurred. She'd had dreams about tasting him, sucking him deeply into her mouth and swallowing his cum. It was another first that she wanted to experience with him while she could. "What can I do to help?" she murmured, transfixed by the sight of his slowly pumping hand and the sound of his ragged breathing.

"Anything," he growled. "Just…please…hurry up and do it."

The bead of pre-cum on the tip of his penis swelled and then rolled sideways across the smooth flesh of his glans, creating a milky trail down the side of his shaft. The tip of Elise's tongue darted out to chase the creamy droplet back the way it had come.

"Ahhhh…" Broderick cried when her flickering tongue lit on his flesh. "Ssssss…"

His sighs and moans were like an incantation to Elise, putting her under a hedonistic spell that completely erased her inhibitions, replacing them with wants and needs and desires that overshadowed reasoning. Emboldened by his hoarse moans, she looked up, saw his hooded gaze watching her, and let her eyes slide closed on an airy sigh as her lips closed around the head of his shaft and slowly descended down its thick length.

Through hooded eyes, Broderick watched Elise's plump, glistening lips bob up and down on his cock and willed himself not to explode in her mouth.

Not yet, he told himself as his hips pumped in time with her wet mouth. *Not yet. God, not yet.*

He loved oral sex, both giving and receiving it. As if it turned her on just as much, she hummed deep in her throat as she sucked him greedily, her eyes half-closed in visible ecstasy. He was mesmerized by the sight of her swaying breasts and her round, full butt tooted up in the air at the foot of the bed.

She took more of his length down her throat and his hips bucked off the mattress. "Oooh, baby, you'll make me cum," he whispered on a shuddering breath. He lifted a hand from the mattress and framed her jaw, gently holding her hair back from her face and feeding himself to her at the same time. "You'll make me… ahhhh!"

He came suddenly, violently, every muscle in his body stiffening as she swallowed his squirting essence greedily. When the sensations shooting through him became too raw to bear another second of her generous mouth, he pulled away and reached for her. Dragging her up the length of his shuddering body, he brought them face-to-face and stared up into her wide, golden eyes. She looked just as stunned as he felt.

"Hi," she whispered against his lips.

"Hi," he whispered back. "I missed you." She giggled and he thought, *I missed that sound, too.*

"Really?"

"Yeah," he said, realizing in that very moment that it was the truth.

"I missed you, too," Elise admitted softly, color staining her cheeks. "I was thinking about you when I walked in here and suddenly—" she paused to swipe her tongue across the seam of his lips "—there you were."

He ran his hands up the slope of her warm back and pushed his fingers into the midst of her silky hair, cupping the back of her head gently. His eyes steady on hers, he sucked her bottom lip inside his mouth and released it slowly, rocking his hips against hers down below. He was hard again. "Really?"

"Yes."

Broderick rolled them over on the mattress and pinned Elise underneath him. Slipping a foil packet from underneath a pillow on the bed, he tore it open and quickly sheathed himself. Then he drove his cock so deeply into her slick tunnel that she cried out. "Damn, you feel good," he said through gritted teeth, holding himself completely still. She was as tight as a fist, spasming around him like a live wire as he stretched her wider and wider. "Am I hurting you?"

She shook her head and dug her fingernails into his butt cheeks, crying out again when he titled his pelvis into hers. "Oh, God, no," she panted up into his face. "More… I want more…please."

"Your wish is my command." Bracing himself on his hands at either side of her head, his hips began moving against hers in an uncoordinated rhythm that shook the bed with its intensity. Without breaking stride, he dipped his head, sucked one of her juicy nipples inside his mouth and took her on the ride of a lifetime.

Chapter 14

"Wake up, Sleeping Beauty."

Buried underneath a pile of sheets, covers and pillows, Elise stirred at the sound of Broderick's deep voice. Her eyes opened one at a time and slowly came into focus as she stretched and yawned until every muscle in her body went limp. Somewhere in the room, Broderick chuckled and the sound was like a direct hit to her clitoris.

Fighting her way out of her cave, she pushed her hair out of her face, rolled over and ran right into his hard chest. "Oh." His face was inches from hers. "Is it morning already?"

"It is somewhere. Here, it's almost midnight and I'm starving. I ordered pizza a few minutes ago, so it should be arriving soon. Are you hungry?"

"A little." She wiggled around in the cocoon of sheets that she'd somehow wrapped herself in and succeeded in freeing her legs and feet. "What time do you have to leave?"

"Eight." He dropped a soft kiss on her lips and pushed his nose into the warm spot in the crook of her neck. "Why?" he wondered, inhaling deeply. "Are you coming with me?"

"To Argentina? Please. As tempting as that sounds, unless there's a new luxury resort there that I don't know about—and, trust me, I know about *all* of them—I'm going to have to pass." Oh, but boy, was she tempted.

"Sorry, but I won't be looking for resorts while I'm there," Broderick said, pressing a wet kiss to the sweet spot just behind her ear and pulling back to look down into her eyes. "What about after I return, though? You think you might be up for another road trip with me then?"

Surprised into speechlessness, Elise's mouth worked for several seconds but no sound emerged. "Um…" She cleared her throat and tried again. "I'm not sure I understand the q-question," she finally managed. "Are you asking me to go away with you?"

"Elise, I just bought a little villa in the South of France that I've been meaning to visit. I have a beach house down in Key West, and a yacht that we could live on for months at a time, without ever having to come ashore. All you have to do is say yes."

He was so down-to-earth and unpretentious that it was easy to forget that he was a very wealthy man. A multimillionaire, if Google could be trusted. "What about work? We can't just drop everything and run off together."

"Can't we?" He cocked a brow, searching her eyes. "I'll take some time off. You'll take some time off. And we'll go somewhere together and figure out exactly what the hell this is that we're doing, because I think we both know that there's more here than just a *fling*. Does that sound like something you'd be interested in doing?"

"Yes," Elise said without hesitation. "Yes, I'd like to but…" *But I know where your sister is and why you haven't been able to find her, and I can't tell you. Right now, right this very second, she's living in an apartment in Dayton, Ohio, and calling herself Emma Deloch, and I can't tell you. And if you knew that I knew and kept it from you anyway, you might feel very differently.*

"But?"

"But… I need to think about it," she said, stalling, her heart thumping in her chest. "This is kind of a big step for me." That, at least, was the truth.

"For me, too," Broderick admitted, flashing her a lopsided grin that was almost bashful. "The last time I went away for any length of time with a woman, I was twenty-four and that woman was my sister. Technically, she doesn't count so you'd be my first." He kissed her. "Just something to think about. Now, come on, let's eat."

Forty-five minutes later, Elise scooped up a third slice of pepperoni pizza, bit into its cheesy goodness and chewed thoughtfully. Setting the slice down inside the greasy box, she wiped her mouth and fingers with a paper napkin and leaned across the bed to grab her wineglass from the nightstand. "Where did you go?" she asked, sipping.

Broderick, who'd already eaten three slices of pizza in the time that it'd taken her to get halfway through her second slice, looked up from typing on his laptop and stared at her over the rim of the dork glasses that he'd magically produced from an inside pocket of his suit jacket. He looked like such a geek that Elise wanted to jump his bones all over again. "Where did I go when?"

"You said that the last time you went away with a woman, it was with your sister. Where did you two go?"

"We went to Hawaii. Her husband had beaten her pretty badly again and she wanted to get away for a while. We were there for a week and as soon as we got back, she went back to him." He turned his attention back to his laptop.

"You didn't like her husband."

"He beat my sister senseless and nothing I said to her *or* did to him was enough to make her leave him. So, no, I didn't like him very much and, as you might expect, the feeling was entirely mutual. She made me promise not to kill him. That's the only reason he died in a car accident, instead of with my fingers wrapped around his throat. I detest men who abuse women."

"Good to know," Elise said, stretching out on the mattress in nothing but Broderick's giant dress shirt and a thong. They were the only things she'd bothered to put on after showering. As soon as the pizza was delivered, they brought it and a bottle of Chianti up to her room to pig out. Now they were camped out in the middle of her bed, with a greasy pizza box and his laptop between them, and she couldn't have imagined a better way to spend her evening if she'd tried. "What about your sister?"

His eyes found hers again. "What about her?"

"Were the two of you close?"

"Not really. She was already ten years old when I was born, so a sibling connection between us never really happened, especially since we only shared a father and she hated my mother. As a teenager, she was cunning and conniving, always in trouble with the local police for one reason or another, and she lied constantly. We hardly spoke after she left home for college. My parents were killed in a drunk-driving accident the year after I graduated from Brown. After that, I joined the navy and applied to the SEALs program. She chose to wander around from place to place, squandering her share of the inheritance on frivolous things. Then she met her dick of a husband and went over to the dark side completely. We've always kept in touch or at least known how to get in contact with each other, if necessary, but there wasn't a lot of love lost between us back then and there still isn't now."

Elise couldn't help comparing the relationship that he described having with his sister to her relationship with Olivia and feeling sorry for him. She couldn't imagine not having her sister up close and personal in her life. "That's sad," she said after a few seconds. "Really sad. What kinds of things did she do on the dark side?"

"She and her husband stole money from a Russian mobster and landed themselves on his hit list. But, unlike her idiot husband, she managed to disappear before she was killed because of it. Frankly, I wasn't very surprised by what she did. I was just glad my parents weren't alive to witness the fallout from it."

"Is she still on his hit list?"

"It's possible but highly unlikely. I've had previous dealings with Borya Maysak and he's an animal, but he isn't a liar."

"You've spoken to him about your sister?"

"Of course. Like I said, we've had dealings before. If my sister was dead and he had anything to do with it, he wouldn't have hesitated to tell me. We're not friends and we never have been. He stays out of my way and I try to return the courtesy. That's the extent of our relationship."

"Okay, let's assume that Brandy is still out there somewhere. If she's in danger, then you finding her could jeopardize whatever safety that she's managed to find up to that point. Why not just leave her alone and let her stay hidden?"

"Because she's also wanted by the US government for perjury and contempt of court, related to an embezzlement case that she was implicated in not long after she resigned from the Federal Reserve. She's a criminal, Elise, and when I find her, I intend to turn her over to the proper authorities, so she can be dealt with accordingly."

"She's your sister, Broderick. How can you be so ruthless?"

"She's also a thief and liar." He caught her eyes and

held them. "Do me a favor and don't ever lie to me, okay? For me, that's one of the few things that there's no coming back from."

At eight o'clock the next morning, Elise sent Broderick off with a kiss and a promise to think about going away with him, and watched him climb into the passenger seat of an idling black Range Rover. After it cleared the driveway and disappeared from sight, she stepped back inside the house and closed the door, sensing that Olivia was behind her without having to look.

"You're in love with him," Olivia accused.

"Yes, I think so." She rested her forehead against the door's cool surface and sighed. "Where have *you* been all night?"

"I answered the doorbell, took one look at that man's face and knew what he was up to. And, since you've been moping around for the past two days, pining away for Mr. Goodbar, I thought I'd get lost for a little while and give you two some privacy. Have you decided what you're going to do about him?"

"He asked me to go away with him." Turning to face Olivia, she leaned back against the door and pushed her hair out of her face. "I told him I'd think about it."

"Wow." Olivia was smiling from ear to ear. "What are you going to tell him?"

"That I can't go."

Her smile fell. "What? Why the hell not?"

"Because he's not the kind of man who can or will look the other way while I break the law, and I care too much for him to ever ask him to."

"Elise—"

She didn't want sympathy or kind words or tearful apologies right now. "It's fine, really. I'll wait a few days and then send him a text or something and tell him that I don't think we should see each other again." She pushed away from the door and crossed the room, tightening the belt of her robe as she went. "Then this nightmare will finally be over and things can return to normal around here," she said as she disappeared down the hallway.

The Argentinian extraction took three days to complete, so Broderick and his team didn't return stateside until late Monday night. By the time they had completed the transaction, disposed of the rebuilt ex-military chopper that he'd commissioned for the trip and then reached the designated pickup spot, it was almost dawn on the West Coast. And they still had a two-hour drive ahead of them before they could board a Cannon Corp chopper for home.

Back at company headquarters, he parted ways with his team, sending them all home to recuperate from being chased and shot at, and, in Leahy's case, one very close call with a fiery death. Then he took the elevator from the basement to his office on the third floor. Since they were all due back for debriefing first thing in the morning, at which time every single detail of the mission would be scrutinized and picked apart, as well as documented and archived, he should've gone home, too. But he'd gotten into the habit years ago of never allowing his work energy to disturb his home energy, so for the time being, his plan to enjoy an ice-cold beer, while lying in the middle of his king-size bed, watching the sports channel, was on hold. He still had a ways to go in separating the two before any of that could happen.

His assistant, Monique, looked up when the elevator doors opened and he stepped out, looking as if he'd been to hell and back and hadn't cared one bit for the trip. His heavy-duty cargo pants and combat boots were splattered with dried mud, his bulletproof vest had taken a few hits and there was dried blood on both of his sleeves that clearly didn't belong to him. He took in her stunned expression and cracked his first smile in three days. "Damn, do I look that bad?"

"If you have to ask, then you already know you do," she replied, her shrewd brown eyes blinking up at him from behind her massive desk as if the mere sight of him was an offense in itself. She'd been working for him since day one, so this was a familiar routine of theirs. "What can I do to help you look normal again…and to get you off my floors? They were just waxed overnight and, up until a second ago, they were spotless."

"Sorry," he said as he approached her L-shaped wooden desk and helped himself to the rest of her blueberry muffin. "Hold all my calls and, if I happen to have any meetings scheduled for this afternoon or evening, please reschedule them. That would really help me right now. Oh, and after I'm done here, I'll be out for the rest of the day."

"Yes, sir," she said, turning to her computer and consulting the electronic appointment book that was already open on the screen. "You don't have any meetings scheduled, but the Phoenix police chief did call first thing this morning to inquire about the two of you possibly meeting for dinner this evening. I think he may have also mentioned something about his wife making her legendary stroganoff, too, but I'm not certain."

Broderick didn't have to think twice about the invitation. "Decline."

"It would be rude to decline a third time," Monique said sweetly, swiveling in her chair to give him a mother hen glare. She had twenty years in the military, two dead husbands and three grown children under her belt, but sometimes Broderick swore that she was intent on claiming him as her long-lost fourth child.

"All right, Monique. Then please *politely* decline."

"Why are you so difficult?" she called after him as he started down the corridor leading to his office. "What excuse am I supposed to use this time? He's not going to buy you being sick, again."

"Tell him the truth—that I hate stroganoff," Broderick called back before closing his office door behind him. He thought about what he'd just said, then snatched the door open again. "Except when you make it for me, I mean," he added, closing the door on her soft giggle.

On the outside, Cannon Corp looked just like all of the other nondescript warehouses in Arizona's downtown warehouse district. He'd purposely left it that way when he bought the building five years ago and completely gutted its interior. But, thanks to a leggy interior decorator whose creative mind had been just as flexible as her compact little body, as well as input from his own in-house management team, the interior work space was a stylish partnership between the exposed duct work overhead and the glossy concrete floors underneath, with sleek leather and tempered-glass appointments, polished woods, and contemporary artwork all expertly sandwiched in between. It was the perfect marriage between Forbes 500 luxury and Rambo functionality, right down to the heated towel racks, in-floor Jacuzzi, and the oversize brick walk-in shower that he'd had installed in the small apartment off his office, where, coincidentally, he slept more often than not.

Stripping and stepping into the shower now, Broderick switched on the water and turned his face up to the forceful spray. As steam rose around him, the tension in his shoulders began melting and the headache kicking at the base of his skull eased. He rotated his head and released the breath that had been lodged in his throat ever since the moment that he had dragged an eleven-year-old boy through a gunfight to a vehicle that was in the process of driving away when he finally reached it, and physically catapulted them both into its backseat.

If any of that had happened just one second later, they'd both be dead right now. He squeezed his eyes shut and waited for the scalding water to help him forget that.

Now that his son had been successfully retrieved, Delgado himself couldn't be extracted until after tomorrow's sentencing hearing, when he would be quickly smuggled out of the courthouse and immediately taken underground for interception by members of Broderick's team. Delgado's wife had already been strapped into a seat aboard the chopper when Broderick and his team had bailed out and he'd given the order for takeoff. He and Leahy had taken a four-member team along with them and everyone had returned safely, a blessing that they'd all acknowledged once Delgado's wife and kid had been handed off and it was safe to remove the masks that they'd worn throughout the ordeal to conceal their identities on the ground.

The others were probably no closer to home than he was right now. Instead, they were likely all huddled around a table in a bar someplace, drinking themselves silly and reminiscing about life before kids, spouses and drug cartels. Another time, he might've been right there with them. But not today.

Today he wasn't in the mood for anything or anyone except Elise.

They hadn't spoken since last week, when he'd left her standing on her porch with her hair standing all over her head, a quarter-sized hickey staining the column of her neck and a question to consider. Per the standard protocol for extractions, he had gone into blackout status before leaving for Argentina, which meant that he'd suspended all communication with the outside world until the mission was completed and he was safely back on North American soil. But now that he was, he was ready to hear her response.

Dressed in navy linen trousers and a navy collarless shirt, and feeling slightly more human now that he actually looked it, Broderick grabbed a yogurt from the fridge in the kitchen and padded barefoot back out into his office to boot up his interface and plug back in to the world.

As if she'd been timing him, Monique's voice came

through the speakerphone on his desk as soon as he crossed the threshold. "Excuse me, Mr. Cannon, but I was so distracted by your Crocodile Dundee getup earlier, that I forgot to mention that there was a package delivered by courier for you the other day. Saturday afternoon, I believe. The weekend receptionist downstairs signed for it and sent it through security. They brought it up this morning. I can bring it right in to you now, if you like."

"Please do," he said, dropping into the leather captain's chair behind his desk and pressing a button to open up his work email account on the computer screen in front of him. He scanned the list of messages in his inbox while he waited, seeing none that required his immediate attention until he scrolled to the bottom of the list and saw Elise's name attached to a message. Curious to see what she'd written, he opened her message first and began reading.

Broderick,
I sent you a package. It should be there, waiting for you when you return to the office. I'll be gone by then, so don't bother trying to reach me. I'm going away for a while. Alone. So, I guess, there's your answer to the question you asked me. I just thought you should have the information I sent you before I left. I think it'll help you get the justice you seek.

Whatever happens next, thanks for the fling. I think you know how much I enjoyed it and you.
Elise

He looked up when Monique came through the door, carrying a large yellow shipping envelope. Taking it from her and dismissing her with a look, he waited until she was gone to check the return address on the front, tear it open and then dump out its contents on his desktop. After several minutes of looking at photos, sorting through documents and reading the same passages over and over again for clarification, he reached across his desk and buzzed Monique.

"Yes?"

"Send for my car and driver, please, Monique," he said. "And place the jet on standby for a possible evening flight."

Elise Carrington had given him exactly what she'd sworn that she was capable of giving him—the key to his sister's whereabouts. And, if he was reading the information that she'd sent him correctly, she'd had it all along. He was sure that there was more, much more to the story, but he'd seen and read enough to get the gist, which was that the woman he was falling in love with had been lying to him all along.

Elise Carrington was a criminal.

"Where to?" Monique asked.

"Missouri."

Chapter 15

The look on her face turned defiant when she flung the door open and saw him standing on the other side of it. Unlike her twin, her skin didn't flush the moment she saw him and her feline gaze didn't wander away from the intensity of his searching one. Instead, it held on tight and stared him down.

She'd been expecting him.

"Is she here?" Broderick asked Olivia.

"No, but I have a feeling you already knew that. Come in," she said, stepping back and opening the door wider. "I've been expecting you or someone like you to show up for a couple of days now. Did you bring a search warrant and a team of careless lackeys along with you to rifle through my drawers and turn my house upside down, too?"

"No, but I can make a few calls and set things in motion if you like." He stepped inside the house and closed the door at his back. The aroma of something delicious wafted past his nose and his empty stomach complained.

"Don't be pithy, Mr. Cannon."

"I could ask the same of you."

"Touché," she said, flicking a glance at him as she took his coat and hung it in the coat closet. "I was just about to have some seafood gumbo. Would you like to join me? And don't lie because I heard your stomach growling just now."

"In that case, I would love to join you." Falling in step behind her, he followed her down a long hallway to the kitchen at the back of the house. Taking a seat at the island in the center of the room, he took in his surroundings while she moved around the room, opening and closing cabinets and drawers. "Nice house."

"Thank you. My parents had it built about five years ago, right before they packed up and moved to London." She took two bowls from a cabinet and grabbed spoons from the silverware drawer, sending it sliding shut with a denim-clad hip. "Elise and I moved in after they were gone. It's a pretentious showplace, but it allows both of us to live under the same roof without killing each other, so we like it. Wine?" she asked, setting the bowls and spoons down and moving to the refrigerator.

"Do your parents have any idea that their daughters are running a crime syndicate out of their showplace? Yes, I believe I will have a glass of wine, thank you."

"My parents don't have a clue, so let's leave them

out of this, all right?" She poured two glasses of white wine and passed him one. They watched each other sip, and then she set her glass down and stepped up to the sink to wash her hands. Drying them on a dish towel, she glanced back at him over her shoulder. "Maybe we should start at the beginning."

"And where, exactly, would that be, Miss Carrington?"

"At the point where you tell me exactly what it is that you think you know." She smiled sweetly at him. "Where else?"

"All right. I know that you and your sister somehow managed to completely wipe my sister off the map three years ago and that you were so good at it that even I couldn't find her. I know that you and whoever else is involved in your little crime ring is responsible for providing her with a new identity and a new life, and I know that you've done those very same things for countless other women since your sham of an agency opened for business. And I think we both know that all of those things would be classified by any reasonable person as crimes. *Federal* crimes."

"Would you like rice?"

"White or brown?"

"White."

"Yes, please," he replied without missing a beat. "By the way, what is this agency of yours, really? I mean, what else do the two of you do here, besides help fugitives from justice escape captivity? Do you smuggle foreigners into the country for questionable employment or marital opportunities, too? Arrange illegal, transatlantic adoptions for couples who can't conceive? What?" Unsure if he was more outraged or intrigued, he got to his feet and washed his hands at the sink while she topped off their glasses.

"You have it all wrong" was all she said after he resumed his seat and stared at her expectantly.

"Explain it to me, then."

"My sister may be in love with you, Mr. Cannon, but I'm not. I don't have to explain anything to you. Frankly, I don't trust you."

She set a steaming bowl of gumbo in front of him and handed him a linen napkin, seemingly unaware that she'd just dropped a bomb on him and sent his wits flying in a million different directions. He nodded his thanks, draped the napkin across his lap and cleared his suddenly dry throat. *Where the hell was his voice?*

He wasn't sure if knowing how Elise felt about him was a gift or punishment. All the way there, he had gone back and forth with himself about what he planned to do when he arrived. And, until that very moment, he'd been undecided, or at least that's what he'd been telling himself. He wanted to believe that he had traveled all the way to Missouri from Phoenix, in the interest of truth and, eventually, justice. But the truth of the matter was that he could've placed a few phone calls from his desk in Phoenix and accomplished the same thing. No, discovering that the woman he loved was a practicing felon wasn't really why he'd come. The implication that she was done with him was.

He was in love with her.

There, he'd finally admitted it to himself. But could

he look the other way while she committed the kinds of crimes that could land her on Court TV?

"Explain it to me anyway," he said, wanting, needing, to know more.

"The first thing you should know is that Elise and I aren't running a crime syndicate. The majority of our business really does come from the usual stuff—cheating spouses, missing children, will and probate issues, and on and on. I mean, don't get me wrong, our clients do tend to be highbrow, so we've encountered our share of scandals along the way. But nothing about the services we provide to ninety-five percent of them is or ever has been illegal. Taking on your sister's case was a mistake—one that I made on my own. She was an exception to our rules that I wish I'd never made." She sat across from him at the island and draped her own napkin across her lap. They picked up their spoons at the same time and eyed each other suspiciously as they sampled. "How's the gumbo?" Olivia asked after swallowing.

"Superb. You don't seem like the type who knows her way around a kitchen." He wiped his mouth with his napkin and reached for his wineglass.

Olivia's eyebrows shot up, her mouth dropped open. "You're kidding, right? I mean, you aren't really that much of an ass, are you?"

"You'd be surprised."

"Actually, now that you mention it, no, I wouldn't."

They stared at each other.

She held his gaze while she drank from her wineglass, and he had the distinct feeling that she was reading him, assessing his character and possibly finding him lacking somehow. She was smiling, not at him but at something that she'd been thinking just then, when she set her glass down with a soft click and cleared her throat. "You're in love with her, aren't you?"

He thought about lying to her. Then he thought about Elise and couldn't lie to himself. "Yes. Are you going to answer my question?"

"Eventually, but we're getting a little ahead of ourselves. Did I ever tell you about what Elise was like in high school?"

"You know damn well that you didn't." He chewed a chunk of perfectly seasoned crab meat and swallowed slowly. "But I'm all ears now, though."

"Elise was painfully shy," Olivia told him as she sipped from her second glass of wine. She'd gotten better at socializing by the time they reached high school, but her mind was always on other things, like helping women at the shelter where she had volunteered for what seemed like forever.

"That place was her second home," Olivia joked. "It's why she became a police officer in the first place—to help lost souls find their way and blah, blah, blah. But the experience wasn't quite the fairy tale that she hoped it would be. She couldn't stomach the violence and the more she dealt with the victims of violence, the more disillusioned she became. She felt like the justice system was failing abuse victims. So when she was recruited by the marshals, she was more than ready to make the move, if nothing else than to get away from that part of it for a while. She liked it and she was good at it, so..." Olivia paused to take a deep breath and release it slowly. "After she'd been with the Marshals Service for a few years, someone there approached her about coming aboard with the network. They had been watching her for a while. That's when we started."

"The network. What is this network?"

"Just a group of people who help battered women," she said. "Would you like more gumbo?"

"I couldn't eat another bite."

"A slice of caramel cheesecake, then?"

He cocked a brow. "Did you make that, too?"

She cocked a brow right back. "What do you think?"

"I think you're tying to distract me and it's not going to work. I still want to hear about the network."

"You know, you really are overthinking this whole thing," Olivia told him as she left the island in search of cheesecake. "The answer to each of the questions you asked earlier is *no*. We are not and have never been into human trafficking of any kind. The women we help are at the end of their ropes, some of them with injuries so severe that they've barely survived them. Women whose abusive husbands or significant others won't be stopped, seemingly by anything, not by signed divorce decrees or desperate moves in the middle of the night, by the laws on the books or by the police who show up to enforce them." She replaced his empty bowl with a dessert plate topped with a slice of cheesecake. "It goes without saying that each and every incident of domestic violence is serious, but sometimes there are those incidents that require thinking outside the box. Those are the kinds of cases that we take on."

"For example," Broderick prodded.

"For example, just last month, we erased a woman whose hair had been completely burned off when her ex-husband doused her with gasoline and set her on fire. Before that, she moved around to five different states in the three years since their divorce, trying to outrun him, but he found her every time. Setting her on fire was the last straw. Eventually he would've killed her but knowing that wasn't what brought her to us. Do you know what did, Mr. Cannon?"

"No, what?"

"She'd just been diagnosed with a very aggressive form of breast cancer and given a year or two, at most, to live. She wanted to spend whatever time she had left as a free woman. How could we deny her her last wish?"

Neither of them spoke while he ate and she sipped. When he was finished, he wiped his mouth with the linen napkin one last time and came out with the thing that was bothering him the most. "It's not that I don't understand what you're telling me, because I do. But how can you justify committing the crimes that you and Elise are committing by making people disappear? At the very least, we're talking forgery, identity theft, insurance fraud... The list could on and on, if the full scope of what you've done ever comes out."

"What about you, Mr. Cannon? How can you justify the crimes that you commit in the course of your work?"

"Excuse me?" He stood and carried his dessert plate and fork over to the double sink, set them down carefully.

"You were off somewhere in Argentina just recently, right? How many people did you shoot to kill while you were over there? Better yet, how many did you have to kill in order to accomplish your mission?"

He looked away, sighing heavily. "It's not the same thing."

"But it's still a crime, isn't it? And of course it's the same thing. It's against the law to shoot people just because you want something from them, but I don't see you turning yourself in. You play fast and loose with the law every day yourself. What makes you so much better than us?"

"You have no idea what I do."

"Oh, I think I have a pretty good idea. At least enough of an idea to know that not quite all of the means that you employ to accomplish your ends can be justified in a court of law. If you were an ordinary Joe Schmoe, instead of a government-sanctioned mercenary, they'd have built a special prison just for you and others like you a long time ago. If you think I'm going to stand here and be lectured by you, you're mistaken. And you're a hypocrite. I don't take direction from hypocrites."

"So, what, you think I should just walk out of here and pretend like I don't know what you do?"

"You didn't bring the police or the FBI here with you. Why is that?"

He crossed his arms and glowered at her. "Because I wanted answers first."

"And I just gave them to you. Helping your sister was my mistake. Elise had nothing to do with it and she didn't know anything about it until she got back from the trip to Columbia, Missouri, with you. And, as you can probably surmise from her absence right now, she didn't take the news very well. So I'm asking you right now, flat out, what are your intentions with her?"

Broderick answered Olivia's question with one of his own. "You weren't surprised to see me. How did you know I'd come?"

"The minute that Elise suddenly packed up and rode off into the sunset, I knew what she'd done. I figured it wouldn't be long before you showed up with the police in tow."

"Why didn't you run, too?"

"Because I haven't done anything wrong and, even if I had, I'm not afraid of you. Do you think that my sister and I haven't already prepared ourselves for a situation just like this?"

"Where did she go?"

"Why should I tell you? What are you going to do, have her arrested and extradited back here to face charges?"

"You do know that I could find her with or without your help, don't you?"

The look she gave him was both smug and petty at the same time. "Could you, Mr. Cannon? Could you, *really*? I don't know where she is. She wouldn't tell me and I was trying to give her a few more days to herself before I broke down and had Eli track her down." Her expression turned wary when he took out his cell and pressed a button. She snatched it from him and ended the call that he'd been in the process of making.

"Olivia, I swear to God—"

Holding his cell phone out of his reach with one

hand, Olivia held up her other hand defensively. "No, wait, listen to me," she said, quickly sidestepping him before he could lunge at her and then skipping several feet away from him. They danced around in a wide circle. "Elise isn't like the women you're used to dealing with. I'm sure you've already figured that out by now, but, still."

"My phone, Olivia," Broderick growled, reaching for it and almost succeeding in grabbing it from her before she clutched it to her chest and turned her back to him. He wasn't about to breach her personal space, and she knew it. He backed off and took a breath for patience.

"Not yet. Not until you take a few minutes and think about what you're going to do when you find her. If you're planning to hurt my sister in any way, Mr. Cannon, then, I'm telling you right now—just leave her the hell alone."

Broderick cocked a brow. "Or else what?"

"Or else," Olivia said as she slowly turned to face him, "you'll regret it."

"Is that a threat, Miss Carrington?"

"Not at all. It's actually more like a promise. So what's it going to be, Mr. Cannon? Are you in or are you out?"

Finding Elise took Broderick all of five minutes. It was only a matter of scrolling through his cell's recent call history, singling out her personal cell number and attaching a tracking worm to her cell's signal. After that, everywhere she went, she unwittingly took him along with her. Not that she was necessarily hiding, he thought as finished his walk-through of the tiny beach house that she was calling home these days and went to stand at the sliding glass door in the living room. She'd left a minute or two earlier, looking like a million bucks in a white tank top that caressed her breasts like a lover's touch and a brightly colored ankle-length wrap skirt that fluttered in the breeze as she walked. With his mouth watering at the sight of her long, shapely legs peeking out of the split in the front of her skirt and the unmistakable imprint of her erect nipples through her tank top, he soaked in the look of contentment on her face one last time before picking the flimsy lock on the door and inviting himself into her space. She'd paid the rental fees through the rest of the month in advance, which meant that she was at least planning to hide out there for another couple of weeks, but whether or not that actually happened, he decided, was entirely up to him.

In the week since he'd last spoken with Olivia, he had visited his sister in Dayton. She had matured and seemingly changed for the better, and he was happy for her. For the both of them, because, after all these years, it was nice to have what was left of his family present and accounted for in his life. She had no interest in returning to her old life and there had still been the matter of Borya Maysak's stolen money to deal with, but the road they were on now seemed like a good one. Because of their history, shaking off his wariness was proving to be harder than he imagined it would be, but they were making progress every day.

He found the money in an offshore account that

Dortch had opened without Brandy's knowledge. The amount was a drop in the bucket to Maysak but Broderick flew to Russia to personally return it anyway. Smoothing the man's ruffled feathers was difficult, as he'd expected it to be, but after several vodka shots and lewd jokes, they had eventually reached an understanding that had simultaneously put Brandy Cannon Dortch's name at the very bottom of Maysak's hit list and Broderick squarely in the man's debt. Terms had been agreed to and another vodka toast made, after which he had returned to the States with another mark on his soul and a remarkably clear conscience.

Making Brandy's perjury and contempt of court charges go away was simple enough, as well, since both charges were misdemeanors and the case that she'd been implicated in had already been settled out of court. He'd called in a few favors and had the charges quickly and quietly resolved, for which she'd been profusely grateful. It was exactly the closure she needed to finally put her past behind her for good.

Elise, on the other hand, was still a loose end in the entire debacle, and as soon as she returned from wherever the hell she'd sashayed off to, they were going to settle things between them, whether she wanted to or not. He'd given her a week to herself and kept his distance. But he was here now and all bets were off.

The first thing he planned to do was wring her neck for disappearing the way she had and worrying the hell out of him. As soon as he had arrived on the island a few hours ago, he'd taken one look at her hiding place and his imagination had taken off running for the hills.

From the outside, the two-bedroom cottage was shabby-looking and alarmingly close to the ocean's edge. It was also badly in need of a power washing and a security system that could at least keep out a five-year-old. Located on a short stretch of private beach on Florida's Marco Island, it was the absolute last place that he'd have ever expected to find her in hiding, which, no doubt, was part of the allure for someone like Elise. Discovering that its interior was nicely updated, the exact opposite of its exterior, was a relief, if only a small one.

Which brought him around to the second thing that he was planning to do to her when she finally returned.

Screw.

Her.

Brains.

Out.

He had missed the hell out of her.

Grabbing a bottled water from the refrigerator in the tiny kitchen, Broderick took a seat in a corner of the living-room sofa and settled in to wait for his woman.

Chapter 16

Elise sensed Broderick's presence the moment she walked into the house and slid the door closed at her back. She could smell his intoxicating alpha-male scent in the air. Inhaling him, she closed her eyes for the second that it took to settle her nerves, and then she turned her head and opened them to see his face across the room. Her body reacted instantly, readying itself for an erotic assault, even as her brain kicked into overdrive with possibilities that weren't the least bit sexy. The worst of which being...

"Are you here to arrest me?" she asked, setting the canvas shopping bag she carried on a side table and straightening with her arms folded underneath her breasts, a baleful look on her face.

"For someone who's so worried about being arrested,

you certainly didn't run very far or hide yourself very well."

"I didn't run," she corrected, wishing that her voice wasn't so shaky. She swallowed the lump in her throat, drinking in the sight of him greedily. "I just…left."

"Coward."

Her eyes narrowed. "Look, if this is about your sister—"

"You know damn well that this isn't about my sister," Broderick thundered, rolling to his feet and coming toward her. "This is about you and me. You should've told me."

Elise jumped at the lash in his voice but she held her ground. "Maybe so, but don't act like you don't understand why I couldn't. What was I supposed to say? How was I supposed to explain myself to you?"

"How about with the truth?" He didn't stop coming until their faces were just inches apart, and she could smell the faint scent of peppermint on his breath.

The urge to jump into his arms was strong but she managed to resist. *Barely.* There was nothing sexier to her than a well-dressed man, and Broderick definitely fit the bill in his flawlessly tailored Brooks Brothers suit. His paisley necktie was expertly knotted and lying against his dress shirt so perfectly that her fingers itched to get tangled up in the silk fabric. And, good Lord, he smelled so damn good that she almost swooned. "The truth is complicated," she said, watching his Adam's apple bob in his throat and telling herself to get a grip.

"There are people out there who think that what I do is wrong and you could be one of them."

"What you do *is* wrong."

She waved a dismissive hand. "You won't get an argument from me, because I happen to agree with you," she said as she massaged the wrinkles out of her forehead with stiff fingers. "Technically, you're right. It is illegal." She searched his eyes. "But did you know that, just last year alone, the percentage of women who were killed by their domestic partners dropped from forty-three percent to thirty-one percent? That's a very significant decrease and I'm positive that I had something to do with it. So if you came here, expecting me to say I'm sorry or that I'm ashamed of myself, then you wasted a trip."

"I didn't ask you to apologize."

"Good, because I won't."

They stared at each other.

"I'm just wondering if you realize that there are probably legal ways to do what you're doing."

"*Probably* being the key word," Elise rebutted, grabbing her shopping bag and walking off with it. "Please tell me that you didn't come all the way down here just to give me a lecture on the relationship between morals and legalities," she said over her shoulder as she turned a corner into the kitchen. "Because, as much as I hate to be the one to break it to you, the fact is, sometimes there is no relationship."

He turned the corner behind her and leaned in the doorway. She caught his eyes as she took a carton of milk and salad fixings out of the shopping bag and set them inside the refrigerator. "I help women who have nowhere else to turn. That's all I care about and that's the only reason I do it." Aware of his steady gaze, she moved around the kitchen, putting away the rest of the groceries and neatly folding the shopping bag. He was quiet—too quiet. "What are you thinking?"

"That I've missed you."

She wilted with pleasure, heat simultaneously flooding her face and neck. "You could've called."

"I was in Argentina, on blackout. But I thought about you every day and every night. You're blushing."

"Stop trying to distract me with sex."

His expression turned thoughtful. "Is that all we've been doing, Elise? Just having sex?"

Elise watched him carefully, wondering exactly what he was asking and exactly how she should answer. Was this a trick question? "I'm not sure—" She paused and swallowed nervously. "I mean, I don't know what you mean."

"No?" Coming away from the doorway, he shrugged out of his suit jacket and draped it across the back of one of the bar stools lined up at the breakfast counter. Then he pushed his hands in his trouser pockets and strolled in her direction purposefully. "Why don't I explain it to you?"

The closer he came, the wider Elise's eyes grew. "What are you doing?" Taking a step back, she put up her hands to hold him at bay. "Broderick—" She took another step back and collided with the rim of the sink. "I don't want to play games with you about this. If you're here to arrest me, I have no intention of sleeping with you one last time before you do. Let's just get this over with, okay?" He stopped walking and she held her breath, waiting for the other shoe to drop. He was towering over her now and there was nowhere for her to run. "Well?" she prodded when, instead of pouncing on her, he just stood there, staring at her.

"Elise, if I wanted you in handcuffs, there was no need for me to drag my ass all the way down to Florida to make that happen. I could've just as easily sent the FBI out here to this secluded little shack of yours and saved myself the trouble."

"Why didn't you?"

"Because your sister was right. It would've been hypocritical of me."

At the mention of Olivia, concern creased Elise's face. "My sister? You talked to Olivia?"

"I went there first, looking for you after I received the package you sent me."

"Is she all right? You didn't—"

"No, I didn't and she's fine. She was also right when she pointed out to me that our work—yours and mine— is more alike than I've given it credit for. That doesn't mean that I agree with *how* you do what you do, but I'm not exactly in a position to sit in judgment of it, either." He took his hands out of his pockets and filled them with her butt, applying just enough pressure to bring her shuffling the remaining few inches toward him and landing against his chest softly. "I didn't come here to arrest you, baby. I came here to do this…"

Elise welcomed his kiss with something like greed, loving the way his tongue boldly invaded her mouth and stroked hers seductively. She wrapped her arms around his neck and pulled him closer, opening her mouth wide and moaning when he took the kiss even deeper. She was breathing hard and his very impressive erection was pressing into her abdomen when they finally drew apart.

"You're not angry?"

"Oh, I'm angry all right, but not for the reasons you think. Another time, I'd definitely like to revisit this 'network' scenario that Olivia mentioned, but not right now. Right now, I just want to be with you." The tip of her tongue darted out to moisten her lips and a growl rumbled deep in his throat. "Do you have any idea how beautiful you are?"

"You're just saying that because you want sex," she teased as she slipped a hand between them and squeezed the erection tenting the front of his trousers.

"I intend to get it, too," he murmured, dropping a kiss on her lips. "But I think we both know that there's more happening between us than just sex, and there has been ever since the day you left me no choice but to crash into your car. I didn't think to ask before but, is there someone else in your life, Elise? Someone that *I* need to make disappear?"

"No," she said, blushing. "Why are you just now asking?"

"Because we've started something that I'd like to finish, and I have no intention of sharing you."

"Neither do I."

"Good, then we understand each other." His mouth came for hers again.

"W-wait," Elise stammered, pushing halfheartedly at his chest and praying for the strength to keep her panties on for just a little while longer. Before she got lost in his kisses, there was one other thing that they needed to straighten out between them. "We still have some unfinished business between us that needs to be settled, Broderick."

Broderick's eyebrows shot up, silently inviting her to go on.

She cleared her throat delicately. "I'd like to go on record right now as the winner of our little bet, which *means*..." she trailed off, angling coy looks up at him from beneath thick lashes. "Well... I think *you* know what it means."

He grinned. "You want the Hummer."

"That *was* our agreement. But...if you want to renege, I'll understand."

His grin turned into a full-fledged laugh. "No, you won't, but it's cool. I'm a man of my word and, since I *did* agree to the bet, and *technically*, you did win said bet, the Hummer is yours. But you should know that it comes as part of a package deal."

"Which means?"

"Which means that, if you want it, you have to take me with it."

"I don't recall you mentioning that as part of the terms before."

"I wasn't falling in love with you then." The wicked gleam in his eyes sent a shiver through Elise's body. Already simmering with arousal, she gasped when his large hands glided up her back and massaged her neck and shoulders just the way she liked. Her eyes drifted closed and a moan of pleasure slipped out of her mouth. "Or maybe I was, and I just didn't realize it at the time."

Summoning the strength to step out of the circle of his arms, Elise pulled her tank top up over her head and let it fall to the kitchen floor. Watching him watch her breasts, she untied the knot at her waist and dropped her skirt, too. Naked, except for a white lace excuse for a thong, she reached for his hands and put them on her breasts, where they immediately began kneading her flesh and toying with her tight nipples. "Why don't you take care of these while I take care of this?" she suggested, pausing to enjoy the play of his fingertips against the tips of her nipples before undoing his tie and the buttons down the front of his shirt. She tugged his shirttail and undershirt free, then switched her attention to his belt buckle and zipper. "And this," she murmured when his long, thick penis bobbed free of the slit in the front of his boxers and saluted her. Her fingers curled around it reverently, stroked it rhythmically.

"Ahhh, baby, you make me feel so good. Damn, I've missed you," Broderick growled, his hips pumping in time with her strokes. She tipped her head back and offered him her tongue, drawing him into a wild, hungry kiss that left her dangling on the edge of orgasm.

She tore her mouth away from his. "I've missed you, too."

"Two weeks is a long time. I can't wait any longer," he murmured against her lips, as he captured her hands in his and stilled them on his shaft. "Take me to bed and show me how much you've missed me."

"Gladly."

The living room was as far as they got. There, Broderick cupped Elise's breasts from behind, ground his iron-hard erection into the valley between her butt cheeks and then bent her over the back of the couch. Elise felt the bulging head of his penis stretching the entrance to her slippery tunnel wide and her eyelids dropped like shutters. Unable to breathe, to make a sound, to do anything except *feel* as he sank his shaft inside her over and over again, she went completely still as sensation after sensation rocked her body from head to toe. With one last, deep stroke, he triggered an orgasmic burst that shook her all the way down to her soul. She collapsed over the back of the couch limply, cumming with a hoarse scream that left her throat raw.

Six Months Later

It was raining and the temperature had dropped steadily over the last few hours, resulting in an unusually chilly September night in Sin City. But neither Broderick nor Elise noticed the rain or the chill as they stumbled, hand-in-hand, out of the *Blue Suede Shoes* 24-Hour Wedding Chapel, wearing matching *can you believe we just eloped?* expressions and grinning like idiots.

Throughout the entire ceremony—all thirty cheesy minutes of it—Elise could do little more than stare at the four-carat, princess-cut diamond ring on her finger in amazement. She and Broderick had been like shadows for the past six months. When had he found time to shop for a ring without her suspecting that he was up to something? During their cruise to St. Thomas on his motor yacht? While they were working a kidnapping-for-ransom case in New Orleans? In London for her father's annual birthday bash? In between the two extortion cases in DC that they had wrapped up just last week? How long had he been carrying it around with him, waiting for the right time, and how had he known exactly what she would've chosen for herself?

"What did we just do?" Elise shrieked as they raced hand in hand through the rain to the taxi that was waiting for them at the curb. "I can't believe I just got married in jeans, by Elvis Presley! Olivia is going to kill *me* and my father is going to kill *you*!"

"They'll have to wait until after we get back from South Africa to do it," Broderick replied, smiling as he ushered her into the backseat and then climbed in after her. "We can explain to everyone all about how I couldn't wait another second to make you my wife as soon as we get back and they can all read us the riot act then. Right now, we have a plane to catch. The airport, please," he told the driver.

The cab lurched forward, merging smoothly with the Friday night 3:00 a.m. traffic. Elise moved closer to Broderick in the backseat and rested a hand on his thigh. "I think we should get our stories straight for when someone asks why we suddenly decided to elope. It's bound to happen, so we should be prepared."

He grinned. "I don't know about you, but I plan on telling the truth to anyone who'll listen. You suck at playing *Truth or Dare?* and you lost a dare." He put up a hand when she sputtered indignantly. "Calm down, baby. I'll add a comedic spin to the story somewhere, we'll all have a good laugh and everything will be fine, you'll see."

"Did you hear what I just said, Broderick? My father is going to kill you."

"Elise, your father drinks light beer, plays squash and refers to the toilet as the *loo*. I can't say that I'm all that worried about my life," he said, chuckling despite the scowl on Elise's face. "Besides, baby, none of this is really as sudden as it seems."

"We jumped up in the middle of the night, hopped on a jet and flew to Vegas to elope! I'm wearing jeans, you're wearing khakis and we had to wait for Elvis Presley to finish his last set of the night before he could marry us! The Village People serenaded us with a Luther Vandross song and then Chuck Berry threw rice in my hair on our way out the door! I loved every minute of it but come on now. No one could've *possibly* planned what just happened. I don't think we're going to be able to sell that story. Like I said, we need to come up with a cover story." By the time she was finished, he was silently cracking up. She watched him suspiciously, struck with a sudden thought. "Unless…" she said, trailing off as her eyes narrowed on his gorgeous but guilty-looking face. "Babe…now that I'm thinking about it, exactly how is it that you just *happened* to have a diamond ring in your pocket?"

"Olivia and I picked it out when the three of us were in London for your father's birthday," he admitted, still laughing. "Right after I asked him for his blessing and he gave it to me. I've known since then that I was going to make you my wife, baby, and so has your family. So relax, everything is under control, I promise."

"Oh." Pleasure, mingled with a sharp zing of arousal, fluttered through Elise's system. In a few short minutes, they would board his private jet and take off for South Africa, her chosen honeymoon destination, and they would be in the air for twenty-plus hours. Plenty of time for her to show him just how deeply he moved her. Over and over again.

In case he had other plans for their airtime, like working or taking conference calls or sleeping, she snuggled even closer to him and pressed a soft kiss to the side of his neck. In his lap, her hand slid up his thigh and palmed his hardening penis through his pants.

He heard her loud and clear. "Anytime, anyplace, baby. Just say the word," he growled for her ears only. He sucked in a sharp, whistling breath and hummed deep in his throat as he slowly released it. "*Je vous aime,* Elise. You have no idea how much."

"*Je t'aime aussi,*" she replied just as their taxi pulled up to the airport entrance. "I'm about to show you how much."

"Is that a promise?"

"It sure is."

Broderick paid the fare and climbed out first, reaching back inside for Elise's hand. "Are you ready for our next adventure, Mrs. Cannon?"

"Oh, yeah," Elise said, taking his hand and stepping out of the taxi. "Let's go, Mr. Cannon."

* * * * *

REQUEST YOUR FREE BOOKS!

2 FREE NOVELS
PLUS 2 FREE GIFTS!

KIMANI™
ROMANCE

Love's ultimate destination!